The
ISLAND
of
ADVENTURE

First published by Macmillan in 1944, Enid Blyton's classic story of adventure never ceases to thrill and delight.

For Philip, Dinah, Lucy-Ann, Jack and Kiki the parrot the summer holidays in Cornwall are everything they'd hoped for. Until they begin to realise that something very sinister is taking place on the mysterious Isle of Gloom – where a dangerous adventure awaits them in the abandoned copper mines and secret tunnels beneath the sea.

*Macmillan Classics: breathing new life
into much-loved children's stories*

The Island of Adventure
by Enid Blyton

Alice's Adventures in Wonderland
by Lewis Carroll

Through the Looking-Glass
by Lewis Carroll

The Jungle Book
by Rudyard Kipling

The Milly-Molly-Mandy Storybook
by Joyce Lankester Brisley

Adventures of the Little Wooden Horse
by Ursula Moray Williams

Gobbolino the Witch's Cat
by Ursula Moray Williams

The Teddy Robinson Storybook
by Joan G. Robinson

With a foreword
by Cressida Cowell

The
ISLAND
of
ADVENTURE

Enid Blyton

Illustrated by Stuart Tresilian

MACMILLAN CHILDREN'S BOOKS

First published 1944 by Macmillan Children's Books

This edition published 2014 as part of the Macmillan Classics series by
Macmillan Children's Books
an imprint of Pan Macmillan
a division of Macmillan Publishers Limited
20 New Wharf Road, London N1 9RR
Associated companies throughout the world
www.panmacmillan.com

ISBN 978-0-230-77070-6

1 3 5 7 9 8 6 4 2

A CIP catalogue record for this book is available from the British Library.

Typeset by Kate Warren
Printed and bound by CPI Group (UK) Ltd, Croydon CR0 4YY

Contents

Foreword   vii

1   The Beginning of Things   1

2   Making Friends   13

3   Two Letters – and a Plan   26

4   Craggy-Tops   38

5   Settling in at Craggy-Tops   50

6   The Days Go By   63

7   An Odd Discovery   74

8   In the Cellars   87

9   A Strange Boat   99

10 Night Adventure   112

11 Bill Smugs   125

12 A Treat – and a Surprise for Joe   138

13 Joe Is Tricked Again   150

14 A Glimpse of the Isle of Gloom   162

15 A Peculiar Happening – and a Fine Trip 184

16 Strange Discoveries   201

17 Joe Is Angry   214

18 Off to the Island Again   225

19 Down the Copper Mines   244

20 Prisoners Underground   256

21 Escape – But What About Jack?   268

22 A Talk with Bill – and a Shock   281

23 Another Secret Passage   292

24 A Journey Under the Sea   305

25 An Extraordinary Find   318

26 A Bad Time – and a Surprising Meeting   331

27 A Lot of Things Are Made Clear   343

28 Trapped   355

29 All's Well That Ends Well   371

    About the Author   385

Foreword

When I was a child, I was forbidden by my mother to read books by Enid Blyton. I had no idea why. As far as I was concerned, my mother was new to the mothering business, and therefore full of unreasonable and whimsical notions that time, and more children, would later wear down.

Of course, my mother's prohibition had the predictable effect of making Enid Blyton's books even more irresistibly attractive than they already were, and it was my clear duty as a child (a *Quest*, even) to set about reading as many of the books as I possibly could.

I took this duty very seriously.

Secretly, I checked the books out from the library, I borrowed them from friends, I bought them second-hand with my own pocket money and I read them under the covers. The fact that they were forbidden delights only added to the enjoyment. I read every single Enid Blyton book that I could possibly get my hands on.

I loved them.

Like so many, many children before and after me, Enid Blyton's books played a crucial role in turning me into an avid reader.

When I began, with The Secret Seven, I was still struggling with the mechanics and the puzzlements and the effort of reading. By the time I had made my way through The Five Find-Outers, The Famous Five, Mistletoe Farm, The Naughtiest Girl, the St. Clare's, the Malory Towers and the Adventure series, just to name a few, I was a fully-fledged, confident reader with a love of books.

My mother had entirely missed the point of Enid Blyton.

But then, Enid Blyton wasn't writing to please mothers, or indeed, as she said herself, any critic over the age of twelve.

She was writing to please children.

She could tap into children's dreams, children's

desires, children's wishes, with extraordinary accuracy. She knew that however well behaved and well cared for they might look on the outside, inside they secretly longed for riot and adventure, to be the naughtiest kid in the school, to catch gangs of burglars entirely on their own, to find imaginary worlds at the top of an ordinary-looking tree.

Her books were already thirty years old, so they came from a time of social attitudes and mores that were a world away from my own.

But she had a magical instinct for writing the kind of books that children actually wanted to read.

By the time I was twelve I could discuss the entire Blyton oeuvre with the in-depth knowledge of a mini-academic.

And my favourite out of all of the books was *The Island of Adventure*.

Lucy-Ann and Jack both have red hair, and only Enid Blyton and children under the age of twelve know why having red hair is strangely appealing. Philip owns a menagerie of small animals, and so he always has a mouse poking out of his sleeve, or a hamster in his pocket. I spent hours imagining I was as lucky as this book-child, taking small invisible rodents out of my shirt, stroking them and putting them back again. I even gave these little ghost-mice names.

And then there was Kiki, Jack's white talking parrot. Oh, how I longed for a talking parrot of my own, as beautiful, as funny, as deliciously rude as Kiki! Kiki's rudeness, Kiki's insults, Kiki's blatant naughtiness, were exquisitely and hysterically funny.

When eventually I came to write my own books for children, I tried to write the kind of books that children really want to read, not the kind of books adults would like them to read.

It is important to remember, like Enid Blyton did, that you are writing for the children, not the mothers.

And I realise as I am writing this foreword, that in the Hiccup series my hero has red hair, the action takes place on an island, and Toothless, my little talking dragon who spends a lot of his time snuggled down Hiccup's waistcoat, is even naughtier and more rude than Jack's parrot, Kiki . . .

This was not intentional on my part, but without

knowing it the books that we loved as children become part of our bones and our hearts and our internal landscape without us even realising.

Books have this power.

The Island of Adventure is now seventy years old.

And even after all that time Enid Blyton's books are still inspiring children to become avid readers and to write their own stories.

Children are still programmed to crave adventure, wildness, and to explore. But they spend so much of their lives being supervised and bossed around by adults. They have less freedom now, perhaps, than at any time in history.

No wonder they still love to read about children who go on adventures, who go to boarding school, thus leaving inconvenient parents behind, who go out in boats unattended, visiting secret islands, catching the bad guys that the police cannot catch . . .

The world changes, but children do not change.

And Enid Blyton knew what children wanted.

Cressida Cowell

1

The Beginning of Things

It was really most extraordinary.

There was Philip Mannering, doing his best to puzzle out algebra problems, lying full-length under a tree with nobody near him at all – and yet he could hear a voice speaking to him most distinctly.

'Can't you shut the door, idiot?' said the voice, in a most impatient tone. 'And how many times have I told you to wipe your feet?'

Philip sat up straight and took a good look round for the third time – but the hillside stretched above and below him, completely empty of any boy, girl, man or woman.

'It's so silly,' said Philip to himself. 'Because there is no door to shut, and no mat to wipe my feet on. Whoever is speaking must be perfectly mad. Anyway, I don't like it. A voice without a body is too odd for anything.'

A small brown nose poked up out of Philip's jersey collar. It belonged to a little brown mouse, one of the boy's many pets. Philip put up a gentle hand and rubbed the tiny creature's head. Its nose twitched in delight.

'Shut the door, idiot!' roared the voice from nowhere, 'and don't sniff. Where's your handkerchief?'

This was too much for Philip. He roared back.

'Shut up! I'm not sniffing. Who are you, anyway?'

There was no answer. Philip felt very puzzled. It was uncanny and peculiar. Where did that extraordinary voice with its rude commands come from, on this bright, sunny but completely empty hillside? He shouted again.

'I'm working. If you want to talk, come out and show yourself.'

'All right, Uncle,' said the voice, speaking unexpectedly in a very different tone, apologetic and quiet.

'Gosh!' said Philip. 'I can't stand this. I'll have to solve the mystery. If I can find out where the voice comes from, I may find its owner.' He shouted again. 'Where are you? Come out and let me see you.'

'If I've told you once I've told you a dozen times not to whistle,' answered the voice fiercely. Philip was silent with astonishment. He hadn't been whistling. Evidently the owner of the voice must be completely mad. Philip suddenly felt that he didn't want to meet this strange person. He would rather go home without seeing him.

He looked carefully round. He had no idea at all where the voice came from, but he rather thought it must be somewhere to the left of him. All right, he would go quietly down the hill to the right, keeping to the trees if he could, so that they might hide him a little.

He picked up his books, put his pencil into his pocket and stood up cautiously. He almost jumped out of his skin as the voice broke out into cackles of laughter. Philip forgot to be cautious and darted down the hillside to the shelter of a clump of trees. The laughter stopped suddenly.

Philip stood under a big tree and listened. His heart beat fast. He wished he was back at the house with the others. Then, just above his head, the voice spoke again.

'How many times have I told you to wipe your feet?'

Then there came a most unearthly screech that made poor Philip drop his books in terror. He looked up into the tree nearby, and saw a beautiful white parrot, with a yellow crest on its head that it worked up and down. It gazed at Philip with bright black eyes, its head on one side, its curved beak making a grating noise.

Philip stared at the parrot and the parrot stared

back. Then the bird lifted up a clawed foot and scratched its head very thoughtfully, still raising and lowering its crest. Then it spoke.

'Don't sniff,' it said, in a conversational tone. 'Can't you shut the door, idiot? Where are your manners?'

'Golly!' said Philip, in amazement. 'So it was *you* talking and shouting and laughing! Well – you gave me an awful fright.'

The parrot gave a most realistic sneeze. 'Where's your handkerchief?' it said.

Philip laughed. 'You really are a most extraordinary bird,' he said. 'The cleverest I ever saw. Where have you escaped from?'

'Wipe your feet,' answered the parrot sternly. Philip laughed again. Then he heard the sound of a boy's voice, calling loudly from the bottom of the hill.

'Kiki, Kiki, Kiki! Where have you got to?' The parrot spread out its wings, gave a hideous screech, and sailed away down the hillside towards a house set at the foot. Philip watched it go.

'That was a boy calling it,' he thought. 'And he was in the garden of Hillfoot House, where I'm staying. I wonder if he's come there to be crammed too. I jolly well hope he has. It would be fine to have a parrot like that living with us. It's dull enough having to do lessons in the hols – a parrot would liven things up a bit.'

Philip had had scarlet fever the term before, and measles immediately afterwards, so that he had missed most of his school-work. His headmaster had written to his uncle and aunt suggesting that he should go and stay at the home of one of the teachers for a few weeks, to make up a little of what he had missed. And, much to Philip's disgust, his uncle had at once agreed – so there was Philip, in the summer holidays, having to work at algebra and geography and history, instead of having a fine time with his sister Dinah at his home, Craggy-Tops, by the sea.

He liked the master, Mr Roy, but he was bored with the other two boys there, who, also owing to illness, were being crammed or coached by Mr Roy.

One was much older than Philip, and the other was a poor whining creature who was simply terrified of the various insects and animals that Philip always seemed to be collecting or rescuing. The boy was intensely fond of all creatures and had an amazing knack of making them trust him.

Now he hurried down the hillside, eager to see if another pupil had joined the little holiday collection of boys to be coached. If the new boy owned the parrot, he would be somebody interesting – more interesting than that big lout of a Sam, and better fun than poor whining Oliver.

He opened the garden gate and then stared in surprise. A girl was in the garden, not a very big girl – perhaps about eleven. She had red hair, rather curly, and green eyes, a fair skin and hundreds of freckles. She stared at Philip.

'Hallo,' said Philip, rather liking the look of the girl, who was dressed in shorts and a jersey. 'Have you come here?'

'Looks like it,' said the girl, with a grin. 'But I haven't come to work. Only to be with Jack.'

Who's Jack?' asked Philip.

'My brother,' said the girl. 'He's got to be coached. You should have seen his report last term. He was bottom in everything. He's very clever really, but he just doesn't bother. He says he's going to be an ornithologist, so what's the good of learning dates and capes and poems and things?'

'What's an— an— whatever it was you said?' said Philip, wondering how anyone could possibly have so many freckles on her nose as this girl had.

'Ornithologist? Oh, it's someone who loves and studies birds,' said the girl. 'Didn't you know that? Jack's mad on birds.'

'He ought to come and live where *I* live, then,' said Philip at once. 'I live on a very wild, lonely part of the sea-coast, and there are heaps of rare sea-birds there. I like birds too, but I don't know much about them. I say – does that parrot belong to Jack?'

'Yes,' said the girl. 'He's had her for four years. Her name is Kiki.'

'Did he teach it to say all those things?' said Philip,

thinking that though Jack might be bottom in all school subjects he would certainly get top marks for teaching parrots to talk!

'Oh no,' said the girl, smiling, so that her green eyes twinkled and crinkled. 'Kiki just picked up those sayings of hers – picked them up from our old uncle, who is the crossest old man in the world, I should think. Our mother and father are dead, so Uncle Geoffrey has us in the hols, and doesn't he just hate it! His housekeeper hates us too, so we don't have much of a time, but so long as I have Jack, and so long as Jack has his beloved birds, we are happy enough.'

'I suppose Jack got sent here to learn a few things, like me,' said Philip. 'You'll be lucky – you'll be able to play, go for walks, do what you like, whilst we are stewing in lessons.'

'No, I shan't,' said the girl. 'I shall be with Jack. I don't have him in the school term, so I'm jolly well going to have him in the hols. I think he's marvellous.'

'Well, that's more than *my* sister, Dinah, thinks

of me,' said Philip. 'We're always quarrelling. Hallo – is this Jack?'

A boy came up the path towards Philip. On his left shoulder sat the parrot, Kiki, rubbing her beak softly against Jack's ear, and saying something in a low voice. The boy scratched the parrot's head and gazed at Philip with the same green eyes as his sister had. His hair was even redder, and his face so freckled that it would have been impossible to find a clear space anywhere, for there seemed to be freckles on top of freckles.

'Hallo, Freckles,' said Philip, and grinned.

'Hallo, Tufty,' said Jack, and grinned too. Philip put up his hand and felt his front bit of hair, which always rose up in a sort of tuft. No amount of water and brushing would make it lie down for long.

'Wipe your feet,' said Kiki severely.

'I'm glad you found Kiki all right,' said the girl. 'She didn't like coming to a strange place, and that's why she flew off, I expect.'

'She wasn't far away, Lucy-Ann,' said Jack. 'I bet

old Tufty here got a fright if he heard her up on the hillside.'

'I did,' said Philip, and began telling the two what had happened. They laughed loudly, and Kiki joined in, cackling in a most human manner.

'Golly, I'm glad you and Lucy-Ann have come here,' said Philip, feeling much happier than he had felt for some days. He liked the look of the red-haired, green-eyed brother and sister very much. They would be friends. He would show them the animals he had as pets. They could go for walks together. Jack was some years older than Lucy-Ann, about fourteen, Philip thought, just a little older than he himself was. It was a pity Dinah wasn't there too, then there would be four of them. Dinah was twelve. She would fit in nicely – only, perhaps, with her quick impatience and quarrelsome nature, it might not be peaceful!

'How different Lucy-Ann and Jack are from me and Dinah,' thought Philip. It was quite plain that Lucy-Ann adored Jack, and Philip could not imagine Dinah hanging on to his words, eager to do his bidding, fetching and carrying for him, as Lucy-Ann did for Jack.

'Oh, well – people are different,' thought the boy. 'Dinah's a good sort, even if we do quarrel and fight. She must be having a pretty awful time at Craggy-Tops without me. I bet Aunt Polly is working her hard.'

It was pleasant at tea-time that day to sit and watch Jack's parrot on his shoulder, making remarks from time to time. It was good to see the glint in Lucy-Ann's green eyes as she teased big, slow Sam, and ticked off the smaller, peevish Oliver. Things would liven up a bit now.

They certainly did. Holiday coaching was *much* more fun with Jack and Lucy-Ann there too.

2

Making Friends

Mr Roy, the holiday master, worked the children hard, because that was his job. He coached them the whole of the morning, going over and over everything patiently, making sure it was understood, demanding, and usually getting, close attention.

At least he got it from everyone except Jack. Jack gave close attention to nothing unless it had feathers.

'If you studied your geometry as closely as you study that book on birds, you'd be top of any class,' complained Mr Roy. 'You exasperate me, Jack Trent. You exasperate me more than I can say.'

'Use your handkerchief,' said the parrot impertinently.

Mr Roy made a clicking noise of annoyance with his tongue. 'I shall wring that bird's neck one day. What with you saying you can't work unless Kiki is on your shoulder, and Philip harbouring all kinds of unpleasant creatures about his person, this holiday class is rapidly getting unbearable. The only one that appears to do any work at all is Lucy-Ann, and she hasn't come here to work.'

Lucy-Ann liked work. She enjoyed sitting beside Jack, trying to do the same work as he had been set. Jack mooned over it, thinking of gannets and cormorants which he had just been reading about, whilst Lucy-Ann tried her hand at solving the problems set out in his book. She liked, too, watching Philip, because she never knew what animal or creature would walk out of his sleeve or collar or pocket. The day before, a very large and peculiarly coloured caterpillar had crawled from his sleeve, to Mr Roy's intense annoyance. And that morning a young rat had left Philip's sleeve on a journey of exploration and had gone up Mr Roy's trouser-leg in a most determined manner.

This had upset the whole class for ten minutes whilst Mr Roy had tried to dislodge the rat. It was no wonder he was in a bad temper. He was usually

a patient and amiable man, but two boys like Jack and Philip were disturbing to any class.

The mornings were always passed in hard work. The afternoons were given to preparation for the next day, and to the writing-out of answers on the morning's work. The evenings were completely free. As there were only four boys to coach, Mr Roy could give them each individual attention, and try to fill in the gaps in their knowledge. Usually he was a most successful coach, but these holidays were not showing as much good work as he had hoped.

Sam, the big boy, was stupid and slow. Oliver was peevish, sorry for himself, and resented having to work at all. Jack was impossible, so inattentive at times that it seemed a waste of time to try and teach him. He seemed to think of nothing but birds. 'If I grew feathers, he would probably do everything I told him,' thought Mr Roy. 'I never knew anyone so mad on birds before. I believe he knows the eggs of every bird in the world. He's got good brains, but he won't use them for anything that he's not really interested in.'

Philip was the only boy who showed much improvement, though he was a trial too, with his different and peculiar pets. That rat! Mr Roy shuddered when he thought of how it had felt, climbing up his leg. Really, Lucy-Ann was the only one who worked properly, and she didn't need to. She had only come because she would not be separated from her brother, Jack.

Jack, Philip and Lucy-Ann soon became firm friends. The love for all living things that both Jack and Philip had drew them together. Jack had never had a real friend before, and he enjoyed Philip's jokes and teasing. Lucy-Ann liked Philip too, though she was sometimes jealous when Jack showed his liking for him. Kiki loved Philip, and made funny crooning noises when the boy scratched her head.

Kiki had been a great annoyance to Mr Roy at first. She had interrupted the mornings constantly with her remarks. It was unfortunate that the master had a sniff, because Kiki spoke about it whenever he sniffed.

'Don't sniff!' the parrot would say in a reproving

tone, and the five children would begin to giggle. So Mr Roy forbade Kiki to be brought into the classroom.

But matters only became worse, because Kiki, furious at being shut away outside in the garden, unable to sit on her beloved master's shoulder, sat in a bush outside the half-open window, and made loud and piercing remarks that seemed to be directed at poor Mr Roy.

'Don't talk nonsense,' said the parrot, when Mr Roy was in the middle of explaining some fact of history.

Mr Roy sniffed in exasperation. 'Where's your handkerchief?' asked Kiki at once. Mr Roy went to the window and shouted and waved at Kiki to frighten her away.

'Naughty boy,' said Kiki, not budging an inch. 'I'll send you to bed. You're a naughty boy.'

You couldn't do anything with a bird like that. So Mr Roy gave it up and allowed the parrot to sit on Jack's shoulder once more. Jack worked better with the bird near him, and Kiki was not so disturbing indoors as out-of-doors. All the same, Mr Roy felt he would be very glad when the little holiday school came to an end, and the four boys and one girl went home, together with the parrot and the various creatures owned by Philip.

Philip, Jack and Lucy-Ann left the big slow-witted Sam and the peevish little Oliver to be company for one another each day after tea, and went off on their own together. The boys talked of all the birds and animals they had known, and Lucy-Ann listened, stumbling to keep up with them as they walked. No matter how far they walked, or what steep hills they climbed, the little girl followed. She did not mean to let her beloved brother out of sight.

Philip felt impatient with Lucy-Ann sometimes. 'Golly, I'm glad Dinah doesn't tag after me like Lucy-Ann tags after Jack,' he thought. 'I wonder Jack puts up with it.'

But Jack did. Although he often did not appear to notice Lucy-Ann and did not even speak to her for some time, he was never impatient with her, never irritable or cross. Next to his birds, he cared for Lucy-Ann, thought Philip. Well, it was a good thing somebody cared for her. She didn't seem to have much of a life.

The three children had exchanged news about themselves. 'Our mother and father are both dead,' Jack said. 'We don't remember them. They were killed in an aeroplane crash. We were sent to live with our only relation, Uncle Geoffrey. He's old and cross, always nagging at us. His housekeeper, Mrs Miggles, hates us to go home for the holidays – and you can tell what our life is like by listening to old Kiki. Wipe your feet! Don't sniff! Change your shoes at once! Where's your handkerchief? How many times have I told you not to whistle? Can't you shut the door, idiot?'

Philip laughed. 'Well, if Kiki echoes what she hears in your home, you must have a pretty mouldy time,' he said. 'We don't have too grand a time either – but it's better than you and Lucy-Ann have.'

'Are your father and mother dead too?' asked Lucy-Ann, her green eyes staring at Philip as unblinkingly as a cat's.

'Our father's dead – and he left no money,' said Philip. 'But we've got a mother. She doesn't live with us, though.'

'Why not?' asked Lucy-Ann in surprise.

'Well, she has a job,' said Philip. 'She makes enough money at her job for our schooling and our keep in the hols. She runs an art agency – you know, takes orders for posters and pictures and things, gets artists to do them for her, and then takes a commission on the sales. She's a very good business woman – but we don't see much of her.'

'Is she nice?' asked Jack. Never having had a mother that he could remember, he was always interested in other people's. Philip nodded.

'She's fine,' he said, thinking of his keen-eyed, pretty mother, feeling proud of her cleverness, but secretly sad when he remembered how tired she had seemed sometimes when she had paid them a flying visit. One day, thought Philip, one day *he* would be the clever one – earn the money, keep things going, and make things easy for his hard-working mother.

'And you live with an uncle, like we do?' said Lucy-Ann, stroking a tiny grey squirrel that had suddenly popped its head out of one of Philip's pockets.

'Yes. Dinah and I spend all our hols with Uncle Jocelyn and Aunt Polly,' said Philip. 'Uncle Jocelyn is quite impossible. He's always buying old papers and books and documents, studying them and filing them. He's making it his life-work to work out the history of the part of the coast where we live – there were battles there in the old days, and burnings and killings – all most exciting. He's writing a whole history – but as it seems to take him a year to make certain of a fact or two, he'll have to live to be four or five hundred years old before he gets a quarter of the book done, it seems to me.'

The others laughed. They pictured a cross and learned old man poring over yellow, musty papers. What a waste of time, thought Lucy-Ann. She wondered what Aunt Polly was like.

'What's your aunt like?' she said. Philip screwed up his nose.

'A bit sour,' he said. 'Not too bad, really. Too hardworked, no money, no help in the house except for old Joe, the sort of handyman helper we've got. She makes poor Dinah slave – I won't, so she's given me up, but Dinah's afraid of her and does what she is told more than I do.'

'What's your home like?' asked Lucy-Ann.

'A funny old place, hundreds of years old, half in ruins, awfully big and draughty, set halfway up a steep cliff, and almost drowned in spray in a storm,' said Philip. 'But I love it. It's wild and lonely and strange, and there's the cry of the sea-birds always round it. You'd love it, Freckles.'

Jack thought he would. It sounded exciting to him. His home was ordinary, a house in a row in a small-sized town. But Philip's house sounded really exciting. The wind and the waves and the sea-birds – he felt as if he could almost hear them clamouring together, when he shut his eyes.

'Wake up, wake up, sleepy-head,' said Kiki, pecking gently at Jack's ear. He opened his eyes and laughed. The parrot had an extraordinary way of saying the right thing sometimes.

'I wish I could see that home of yours – Craggy-Tops,' he said to Philip. 'It sounds as if things could happen there – real, live, exciting things, thrilling adventures. Nothing ever happens in Lippinton, where we live.'

'Well, nothing much happens at Craggy-Tops either,' said Philip, putting the little squirrel back into his pocket, and taking a hedgehog out of another pocket. It was a baby one, whose prickles were not yet hardened and set. It seemed quite happy to live in Philip's pocket, along with a very large snail, who was careful to keep inside his shell.

'I wish we were all going home together,' said

Jack. 'I'd like to see your sister Dinah, though she does sound a bit of a wild-cat to me. And I'd love to see all those rare birds on the coast. I'd like to see your old half-ruined house too. Fancy living in a house so old that it's almost a ruin. You don't know how lucky you are.'

'Not so lucky when you have to carry hot water for miles to the only bath in the house,' said Philip, getting up from the grass where he had been sitting with the others. 'Come on – it's time to get back. You're never likely to see Craggy-Tops, and you wouldn't like it if you did – so what's the good of talking about it?'

3

Two Letters – and a Plan

The next day Philip had a letter from Dinah. He showed it to the others.

'Old Dinah's having a rough time,' he said. 'It's a good thing I leave here soon. It's better for her when I'm there.'

DEAR PHIL [said Dinah in her letter],
Aren't you ever coming back? Not that you're much good for anything except quarrelling with, but still it's pretty lonely here with nobody but Uncle and Aunt and Joe, who's even more strange than before. He told me yesterday not to go out at night down the cliff, because there are 'things' wandering about. He's quite mad. The only 'things' wandering about besides me are the sea-birds. There are thousands of them here this year.

Don't, for goodness' sake, bring any creatures

home these holidays. You know how I hate them. I shall die if you bring a bat again, and if you dare to try and train earwigs like you did last year, I'll throw a chair at your head!

Aunt Polly is making me work awfully hard. We wash and scrub and clean all day, goodness knows what for, because nobody ever comes. I shall be glad when it's time to go off to school again. When do you come back? I wish we could earn some money somehow. Aunt Polly is worrying herself to death because she can't pay some bill or other, and Uncle swears he hasn't got the money, and wouldn't give it to her if he had. I suppose Mother would send more money if we asked her, but it's pretty awful to have her slaving away as she does, anyhow. Tell me more about Freckles and Lucy-Ann. I like the sound of them.

Your loving sister,

DINAH

Dinah sounded rather fun, Jack thought, as he read the letter and gave it back to Philip. 'Here you are,

Tufty,' he said. 'Dinah sounds lonely. Hallo – there's Mr Roy beckoning me. I'll see what he wants. More work, I suppose.'

By the same post had come a letter for Mr Roy, from the housekeeper who looked after Jack's Uncle Geoffrey. It was short and to the point.

Mr Roy had read it with dismay, and then called Jack in to show him the letter. Jack read it, also filled with dismay.

DEAR MR ROY [said the letter],
Mr Trent has broken his leg, and he doesn't want the children back these holidays. He wants to know if you will keep them with you, and he sends a cheque to cover the rest of the time. They can come back two days before school begins, to help me to sort out their clothes.

Yours faithfully,

ELSPETH MIGGLES

'Oh, Mr Roy!' groaned Jack who, much as he disliked his home, disliked the thought of staying on with Mr Roy, and with the peevish Oliver, who was also staying on, even more than the thought of returning to his irritable uncle. 'I don't see why Lucy-Ann and I can't go back – we shan't go near Uncle.'

Mr Roy did not want Jack to stay on any more than the boy himself did. The thought of having that parrot for one day longer than he needed to filled him with horror. He had never in his life disliked anything so much as he disliked Kiki. Rude boys he could deal with, and did – but rude parrots were beyond him.

'Well,' said Mr Roy, pursing up his lips and looking at Kiki with dislike, 'well – I'm sure I don't want to keep you any longer, because it's a pure waste of your time to be here – you haven't learnt a thing – but I don't see what else to do. It's quite plain that your uncle doesn't want you back – you can see he has sent quite a generous cheque to cover the rest of your stay here – but I had other plans. With only Oliver here, I intended to do a little visiting. I wish we could find some place for you to go to, you and Lucy-Ann.'

Jack went back to his sister and to Philip, looking so dismayed that Lucy-Ann slipped her arm into his at once.

'What is it? What's the matter?'

'Uncle doesn't want us back,' said Jack, and explained about the letter. 'And Mr Roy doesn't want us here – so it looks as if nobody loves us at the moment, Lucy-Ann.'

The three children looked at one another. And then Philip had his brain-wave. He clutched at Jack, almost knocking Kiki off her balance.

'Jack! Come back home with me! You and Lucy-Ann can come to Craggy-Tops! Dinah would be thrilled. You could have a fine time with the sea-birds. What about it?'

Jack and Lucy-Ann stared in excitement and delight. Go to Craggy-Tops? Live in an old half-ruined house, with a learned uncle, an impatient aunt, a strange handyman and the sound of the sea all the time? Now that really would be thrilling!

Jack sighed and shook his head. He knew that

the plans of children seldom came to anything when grown-ups had to be consulted about them.

'It's no good,' he said. 'Uncle Geoffrey would probably say no – and Mr Roy would anyway – and your uncle and aunt would just hate to have extra children on their hands.'

'They wouldn't,' said Philip. 'You could give them the cheque that your Uncle Geoffrey sent to Mr Roy, and I bet my aunt would be thrilled. It would pay that bill Dinah talked about in her letter.'

'Oh, Philip – oh, Jack – do let's go to Craggy-Tops!' begged Lucy-Ann, her green eyes shining. 'I'd like it more than anything in the world. We'll be in the way here, Jack, if we stay on, you know we will – and I'm sure Mr Roy will kill Kiki one day if she says any more rude things to him.'

Kiki gave a hideous screech and stuck her head hard into Jack's neck. 'It's all right, Kiki,' said Jack. 'I won't let anyone hurt you. Lucy-Ann, honestly it's no good asking Mr Roy to see if we can go to Craggy-Tops. He thinks it's his duty to have us here, and we'll have to stay.'

'Well, let's go without asking him, then,' said Lucy-Ann recklessly. The boys stared at her without speaking. That was an idea. Go without asking! Well – why not?

'It would be all right if we all turned up at Craggy-Tops together, really it would,' said Philip, though he was by no means certain that it would be all right at all. 'You see, once you were there, my uncle and aunt couldn't very well turn you out, and I could get Aunt Polly to telephone to Mr Roy and explain things to him, and get him to send her the cheque your Uncle Geoffrey sent for you.'

'Mr Roy would be glad to think we had gone,' said Lucy-Ann, thinking what fun it would be to know Dinah. 'Uncle Geoff wouldn't care anyhow. So let's, Jack, do let's.'

'All right,' said Jack, giving way suddenly. 'We'll all go off together. When is your train, Tufty? We'll go down to the station saying that we'll see you off – and we'll hop into the carriage at the last minute and go with you.'

'Oooh!' said Lucy-Ann, thrilled.

'Where's your handkerchief? said Kiki, sensing the excitement, and rocking herself to and fro on Jack's shoulder. Nobody took any notice of her. 'Poor old Kiki,' said the parrot sorrowfully. 'Poor old Kiki.'

Jack put up a hand and fondled the parrot, thinking out ways and means of escape. 'We could wheel my trunk and Lucy-Ann's down to the station the night before, when we take yours,' he said. 'Nobody would notice ours were gone out of the loft. We could buy our tickets then too. Has anyone any money?'

The three of them put their money together. It would probably just buy the tickets. They simply must go off together! Now that they had made up their minds, it was quite unthinkable that anything should be allowed to prevent it.

So they made their plans. The day before Philip was due to leave, his trunk was taken from the loft, and Jack managed to get his down unobserved too. He pushed it into a big cupboard in his room, and Lucy-Ann helped him pack it when no one was about.

'I'll wheel my trunk down to the station on the barrow, sir,' said Philip to Mr Roy. It was the custom to do this, and the master nodded, not taking much notice. He wished Jack and that parrot were going too.

The boys managed to get both trunks on to the barrow without being seen, and set off to the station in great spirits. Escape seemed quite easy, after all. Sam and Oliver did not seem to notice anything. Sam was too excited at leaving for home himself, and Oliver too miserable at the idea of being left behind to bother about anyone else.

The next morning Philip said a polite goodbye to Mr Roy. 'Thank you for all your help and coaching, sir,' he said. 'I think I shall get on well next term now. Goodbye, sir.'

'Goodbye, Philip. You've not done badly,' said Mr Roy.

Philip shook hands with Mr Roy, who drew back a little as a mouse ran out of the boy's sleeve. Philip tucked it back again.

'How can you have those creatures running about

you like that?' said Mr Roy, and sniffed loudly.

'Where's your handkerchief?' said the parrot at once, and Mr Roy glared at it. As usual it was on Jack's shoulder.

'Could I go down to the station with Lucy-Ann and see Philip off?' asked Jack. Kiki gave a squawk of laughter, and Jack gave her a little slap. 'Be quiet! There's nothing to laugh at.'

'Naughty boy!' said Kiki, just as if she knew what mischief was in Jack's mind.

'Yes, you can go down and see Philip off,' said Mr Roy, thinking that it would be nice to get rid of the parrot for a little while. So the children went off together, grinning secretly at each other. Kiki had the last word with Mr Roy.

'Can't you shut the door?' she bawled. Mr Roy gave an exasperated click, and banged the door. He heard the parrot's cackle of laughter as the children went down the road.

'If only I need never see that bird again,' he thought to himself, little knowing that his wish was about to come true.

Jack, Lucy-Ann and Philip arrived at the station in plenty of time. They found their luggage and gave it to the porter to put on the train. When the engine steamed in they found an empty carriage and got in. No one stopped them. No one guessed that two of the children were running away. They all felt thrilled and rather nervous.

'I do hope your uncle and aunt won't send us back,' said Jack, stroking Kiki to quieten her. She did not like the noise of the trains, and had already told one to stop whistling. An old lady looked as if she were about to get into their carriage, but when Kiki gave one of her appalling screeches, she

thought again and hurried a good way up the train.

At last the train moved off, with many snorts that caused the excited parrot to tell it to use its handkerchief, much to the children's amusement. It steamed out of the station, and, in the distance, the children saw the house where they had lived for the past few weeks, sitting at the bottom of the hill.

'Well – we're off,' said Philip, pleased. 'And it was perfectly easy for you to escape, wasn't it? Golly, what fun it will be to have you and Lucy-Ann at Craggy-Tops! Dinah will be thrilled to bits when we arrive.'

'Off to Craggy-Tops!' sang Lucy-Ann. 'Off to the sea and the wind and the waves! Off to Craggy-Tops!'

Yes – off to Craggy-Tops – and to a wild and astonishing time that not one of the children could possibly have imagined. Off to Craggy-Tops – and off to Adventure.

4

Craggy-Tops

The train sped on through the countryside, passing many stations, and stopping at very few. On towards the coast it went, through high mountains that towered up, over silver rivers, through big, straggling towns.

And then it came to wilder country. The sea-wind came in at the window. 'I can smell the sea already,' said Jack, who had only once before been to the sea, and scarcely remembered it.

The train stopped at last at a lonely little station. 'Here we are,' said Philip. 'Tumble out. Hi, Joe! Here I am. Have you got the old car handy?'

Jack and Lucy-Ann saw a strange man coming towards them. His skin was lined, his teeth were very white, and his eyes darted from side to side as he looked at them. Running behind him was a girl a little older than Lucy-Ann, but tall for her age. She had the same brown, wavy hair that

Philip had, and the same tuft in front.

'Another Tufty,' thought Jack, 'but a fiercer one. It must be Dinah.'

It *was* Dinah. She had come with Joe to meet Philip, in the ramshackle old car. She stopped short when she saw Lucy-Ann and Jack. Jack grinned, but Lucy-Ann, suddenly feeling shy of this strapping, confident-looking girl, hid behind her brother. Dinah stared in even greater amazement at Kiki, who was telling Joe to wipe his feet at once.

'You mind your manners,' said Joe roughly, talking to the bird as if it was a human being. Kiki put up her crest and growled angrily, like a dog. Joe looked startled.

'That a bird?' he enquired of Philip.

'Yes,' said Philip. 'Joe, that trunk should go in the car too. It belongs to my two friends.'

'They coming to Craggy-Tops?' said Joe in the greatest surprise. 'Miss Polly, she didn't say nothing about any friends, no, she didn't.'

'Philip, who are they?' asked Dinah, coming up and joining the little group.

'Two friends from Mr Roy's,' said Philip. 'I'll tell you all about it afterwards.' He winked at Dinah to make her understand that he would explain when Joe was not there. 'This is Freckles – I told you about him, you know – and Lucy-Ann too.'

The three children solemnly shook hands. Then they all got into the jerky, jumpy old car, with the two trunks at the back, and Joe drove off in a manner that seemed most dangerous to Lucy-Ann. She clutched the side of the car, half frightened.

They drove through wild hills, rocky and bare. Soon they saw the sea in the distance. High cliffs bounded it except for breaks here and there. It certainly was a wild and desolate coast. They passed ruined mansions and cottages on their way.

'They were burnt in the battle I told you about,' said Philip. 'And no one has rebuilt them. Craggy-Tops more or less escaped.'

'That's the cliff behind which Craggy-Tops is built,' said Dinah, pointing. The others saw a high, rocky cliff, and just jutting up they could see a small round tower, which they imagined was part of Craggy-Tops.

'Craggy-Tops is built out of reach of the waves,' said Philip, 'but on stormy nights the spray dashes against the windows almost as strongly as the waves pound the shore.'

Lucy-Ann and Jack thought it all sounded very thrilling. It would be fun to stay in a house that had spray dashed against its windows. They did hope there would be a terrific storm whilst they were there.

'Is Miss Polly expecting you all?' asked Joe suddenly. He was plainly puzzled by the two extra children. 'She didn't say nothing to me about them.'

'Didn't she? How strange!' said Philip. Kiki screeched with laughter, and Joe wrinkled up his nose in dislike of the noise. He was not going to fall in love with Kiki, that was certain. Jack didn't like the way the man looked at his pet bird.

Dinah suddenly gave a shriek and pushed Philip away from her. 'Oh! You've got a mouse down your neck! I saw its nose peeping out. Take it away,

Philip; you know I can't bear mice.'

'Oh, shut up and don't be an idiot,' said Philip crossly. Dinah at once flew into one of her tempers. She clutched Philip's collar and shook him, trying to dislodge the mouse and frighten it away. Philip gave Dinah a push, and she banged her head against the side of the car. She at once slapped him hard. Jack and Lucy-Ann stared in surprise.

'Beast!' said Dinah. 'I wish you hadn't come back. Take your two horrid friends and go off again to Mr Roy.'

'They're not horrid,' said Philip, in a mild tone. 'They're fun.' He put his mouth to Dinah's ear, after seeing that Joe was paying no attention, and whispered: 'They've escaped from Mr Roy. I asked them to. Their uncle will pay Aunt Polly for them to stay with us, and she can pay that bill you told me about. See?'

Dinah forgot her temper as quickly as it had come. She stared with interest at the brother and sister, rubbing her bruised head as she did so. What would Aunt Polly say? Where would they sleep?

This was going to be exciting.

Joe drove headlong over the bumpy, stony road. Jack wondered that any car could stand such driving. They drove up the cliff, then down a hidden way that sloped round to Craggy-Tops.

And there, suddenly, was the roaring sea and Craggy-Tops standing sullenly above it, built halfway down the cliff. The car stopped, and the children got out. Jack gazed at the house. It was a strange place. Once it had two towers, but one had fallen in. The other still stood. The house was built of great grey stones, and was massive and ugly, but somehow rather grand. It faced the sea with a proud and angry look, as if defying the strong gale and the restless ocean. Jack looked down at the water. On it, and circling above it, were hundreds of wild sea-birds of all kinds. It was a perfect paradise of birds. The boy's heart sang for joy. Birds by the hundred, birds by the thousand. He would be able to study them to his heart's content, find their nests, photograph them at his leisure. What a time he would have!

A woman came to the door, and looked down at the four children in surprise. She was thin, and her hair was sandy-coloured and wispy. She looked tired and faded.

'Hallo, Aunt Polly!' cried Philip, running up the stone steps. 'I'm back!'

'So I see,' said his aunt, giving him a peck of a kiss on his cheek. 'But who are these?'

'Aunt Polly, they're friends of mine,' said Philip earnestly. 'They couldn't go home because their uncle broke his leg. So I brought them here. Their uncle will pay you for having them.'

'Philip! How can you do a thing like this? Springing people on me without telling me!' said Aunt Polly sharply. 'Where will they sleep? You know we've no room.'

'They can sleep in the tower-room,' said Philip. The tower-room! How lovely! Jack and Lucy-Ann were thrilled.

'There are no beds there,' said Aunt Polly, in a disagreeable tone. 'They'll have to go back. They can stay the night and then go back.'

Lucy-Ann looked ready to cry. There was a harshness in Aunt Polly's tone that she could not bear. She felt unwelcome and miserable. Jack put his arm round her and gave her a squeeze.

He was determined that he would not go back. The sight of those gliding, circling, soaring birds had filled his heart with joy. Oh, to lie on the cliff and watch them! He would *not* go back!

They all went in, Joe carrying the trunks. Aunt Polly looked with much disfavour on Kiki.

'A parrot too!' she said. 'Nasty, squawking, screeching bird! I never liked parrots. It's bad enough to have all the creatures you collect, Philip, without a parrot coming too.'

'Poor Polly, poor old Polly,' said Kiki unexpectedly. Aunt Polly looked at the bird, startled.

'How does it know my name?' she asked in astonishment. Kiki didn't. It was a name she herself was often called, and she often said 'Poor old Polly!' or 'Poor old Kiki!' She saw that she had made an impression on this sharp-voiced woman, and she repeated the words softly, as if she was about to burst into tears.

'Poor Polly! Dear Polly! Poor, dear old Polly!'

'Well I never!' said Aunt Polly, and looked at the parrot more kindly. Aunt Polly felt ill, tired and harassed, but no one ever said they were sorry, or seemed to notice it. Now here was a bird pitying her and speaking to her more kindly than anyone had for years! Aunt Polly felt strange about it, but quite pleased.

'You can take a mattress up to the tower-room, and sleep there tonight with the boy – what's his name?' said Aunt Polly to Philip. 'The girl can sleep with Dinah. It's a small bed, but I can't help that. If you bring people here without telling me, I can't prepare for them.'

The children sat down to a good meal. Aunt Polly was a good cook. It was a mixture of tea and supper, and the children tucked into it well. All they had had that day, since their breakfast, were the sandwiches that Mr Roy had packed for Philip – and one packet of sandwiches did not go far between three hungry children.

Dinah gave a sneeze, and the parrot spoke to her sternly. 'Where's your handkerchief?'

Aunt Polly looked at the bird in surprised admiration. 'Well, I'm always saying that to Dinah,' she said. 'That bird seems to be a most sensible creature.'

Kiki was pleased at Aunt Polly's admiration. 'Poor Polly, poor dear Polly,' she said, her head coyly on one side, her bright eye glinting at Aunt Polly.

'Aunt Polly likes your parrot better than she likes *you*,' whispered Philip to Jack, with a grin.

After the meal, Aunt Polly took Philip to his uncle's study. He knocked and went in. His Uncle Jocelyn was bent over a sheaf of yellow papers, examining them with a magnifying-glass. He grunted at Philip.

'So you're back again. Behave yourself and keep out of my way. I shall be very busy these holidays.'

'Jocelyn, Philip has brought two children back with him – and a parrot,' said Aunt Polly.

'A parrot?' said Uncle Jocelyn. 'Why a parrot?'

'Jocelyn, that parrot belongs to one of the children that Philip brought home,' said Aunt Polly. 'Philip wants these children to stay here.'

'Can't have them. Don't mind the parrot,' said Uncle Jocelyn. 'Keep the parrot if you want it. Send it away if you don't. I'm busy.'

He bent over his papers again. Aunt Polly gave a

sigh and shut the door. 'He's so interested in the past that he forgets all about the present,' she said, half to herself. 'Well – I suppose I must ring up Mr Roy myself. He'll be wondering about those children.'

She went to the telephone. Philip followed close behind her, longing to know what Mr Roy would say. Dinah peeped out from the sitting-room and Philip nodded towards the telephone. If only Mr Roy was cross and said he would not have Jack and Lucy-Ann back! If only Aunt Polly would think the cheque was big enough to make it worthwhile letting them stay!

5

Settling in at Craggy-Tops

It seemed ages before Aunt Polly got through to Mr Roy. The master was worried and puzzled. Jack and Lucy-Ann had not returned, of course, and at first he had thought they had gone off for one of their walks, and that Jack had found some unusual bird and had forgotten all about time.

But as the hours went by and still the children had not come back, he became seriously worried. It did not occur to him that they might have gone with Philip, or he would have telephoned to the boy's aunt at once.

He was most relieved to hear Mrs Sullivan, Philip's aunt, speaking, giving him the news that the children were safe.

'They arrived here with Philip,' she said, with some sharpness. 'I cannot think how it was that they were allowed to do this. I cannot possibly keep them.'

Mr Roy's heart sank. He had hoped for one wild moment that his problem concerning Jack and Lucy-Ann, and that tiresome parrot, was solved. Now it seemed as if it wasn't.

'Well, Mrs Sullivan,' said Mr Roy politely, though he did not feel at all civil, 'I'm sorry about it. The children went down to see Philip off, and I suppose the boy persuaded them to go with him. It's a pity you could not keep them for the rest of the holidays, as they would probably be happier with you and Philip. No doubt they have told you that their uncle cannot have them back these holidays. He sent me a cheque for a large sum of money, hoping that I could have them. But I should be pleased to hand this over to you if you felt that you could take charge of them, and we could get Mr Trent's consent to it.'

There was a pause. 'How much was the cheque?' asked Mrs Sullivan.

There was another pause after Mr Roy told her the sum of money that had been sent. It certainly was a very generous amount. Mrs Sullivan thought quickly. The children would not cost much to keep.

She could see that they kept out of Jocelyn's way. That girl Lucy-Ann could help Dinah with the housework. And she would be able to pay off a few bills, which would be a great relief to her.

Mr Roy waited hopefully at the other end of the wire. He could not bear the thought of having the parrot back again. Jack was bearable, Lucy-Ann was nice – but Kiki was impossible.

'Well,' said Mrs Sullivan, in the sort of voice that meant she was prepared to give in. 'Well – let me think now. It's going to be difficult – because we've so little room here. I mean, though the house is enormous, half of it is in ruins and most of it is too draughty to live in. But perhaps we could manage. If I use the tower-room again . . .'

Philip and the others, who could hear everything that was being said by Mrs Sullivan, looked at one another in delight. 'Aunt Polly's giving in!' whispered Philip. 'And oh, Jack – I bet we'll have the old tower-room for our own. I've always wanted to sleep there and have it for my room, but Aunt Polly would never let me.'

'Mrs Sullivan, you would be doing me a great kindness if you could manage to take the children off my hands,' said Mr Roy earnestly. 'I will telephone at once to Mr Trent. Leave it all to me. I will send you the cheque. And if you should need any more money, let me know. I really cannot tell you how obliged I should be to you if you could manage this for me. The children are quite easy to look after. Lucy-Ann is sweet. It's only that awful parrot – so rude – but you could get a cage for it, perhaps.'

'Oh, I don't mind the parrot,' said Mrs Sullivan, which surprised Mr Roy very much. Kiki gave a loud squawk, which Mr Roy heard down the telephone. Well – Mrs Sullivan must be a remarkable woman if she liked Kiki!

Not much more was said. Mrs Sullivan said she would write to Mr Trent, after she had heard again from Mr Roy. In the meantime she undertook to look after the children for the rest of the holidays.

The receiver clicked as she put it down. The children heaved a sigh of relief. Philip went up to his aunt.

'Oh, thanks, Aunt Polly,' he said. 'It will be fine for me and Dinah to have friends with us. We'll try and keep out of Uncle's way, and help you all we can.'

'Dear Polly,' said Kiki affectionately, and actually left Jack's shoulder to hop on to Aunt Polly's! The children stared in astonishment. Good old Kiki! She was playing up to Aunt Polly properly.

'Silly bird!' said Aunt Polly, hardly liking to show how pleased she was.

'God save the Queen,' said Kiki unexpectedly, and everyone laughed.

'Philip, you and Jack must have the tower-room for your own,' said Aunt Polly. 'Come with me, and I'll see what can be arranged. Dinah, go to your room and see if you would rather share it with Lucy-Ann, or whether she would rather have Philip's old room. They open out of one another, so perhaps you would like to have the two rooms.'

Dinah went off happily with Lucy-Ann to examine the room. Lucy-Ann wished she was sleeping nearer to Jack. The tower-room was a good way from where she herself would sleep. Jack took Kiki and went to a high window, settling on the window seat to watch the sea-birds in their restless soaring and gliding outside.

Philip went to the tower-room with his aunt. He felt very happy. He had become very fond of Jack and Lucy-Ann, and it was almost too good to be true to think they had come to stay with him for some weeks.

The two of them went down a cold stone passage. They came to a narrow, winding stone stairway, and climbed up the steep steps. The stairway wound round and round, and at last came out into the tower-room. This was a perfectly round room whose walls were very thick. It had three narrow windows, one facing the sea. There was no glass in it at all, and the room was draughty, and full of the sound of the crying of birds, and the roaring of the waves below.

'I'm afraid this room will be cold for you two boys,' said Aunt Polly, but Philip shook his head at once.

'We shan't mind that. We should have the windows wide open if there *was* any glass, Aunt Polly. We'll be all right. We shall love it up here. Look – there's an old oak chest to put our things in – and a wooden stool – and we can bring a rug up from downstairs. We only need a mattress.'

'Well – we can't possibly get a bed up those narrow stairs,' said Aunt Polly. 'So you will have to have a mattress to sleep on. I've got an old double one that must do for you. I will send Dinah up with a broom and a cloth to clean the room a bit.'

'Aunt Polly, thanks awfully again for arranging all this,' said Philip, half shyly, for he was afraid of his hard-working aunt, and although he spent all his holidays with her, he felt that he did not really know her very well. 'I hope Mr Trent's cheque will cover all your expenses – but I'm sure Jack and Lucy-Ann won't cost much.'

'Well, Philip,' said Aunt Polly, shutting the lid of the old chest and turning to the boy with a troubled face, 'well, my boy, you mustn't think I am making too much fuss – but the fact is, your mother hasn't been at all well, and hasn't been able to send nearly as much money for you as usual – and, you see, your school fees are rather high – and I've been a bit worried to know what to do. You are old enough now to realise that dear old Uncle Jocelyn is not much use in bearing responsibility for a household – and the bit of money I have soon goes.'

Philip listened in alarm. His mother was ill! Aunt Polly hadn't been getting the money as usual – it all sounded very worrying to him.

'What's the matter with Mother?' he asked.

'Well – she's very thin and run-down, and she's got a dreadful cough, she says,' answered Aunt Polly. 'The doctors say she must have a long rest – by the sea if possible – but how can she give up her job?'

'I shan't go back to school,' said Philip at once. 'I shall find a job myself somehow. I can't have Mother working herself to death for us.'

'You can't do that,' said Aunt Polly. 'Why, you are not even fourteen yet. No – now that I have a little money coming in from Mr Trent for these two children, it will ease things a good deal.'

'This house is too big for you,' said Philip, suddenly noticing how tired his aunt looked. 'Aunt Polly, why do we have to live here? Why can't we leave and take a nice little house somewhere, where you wouldn't have to work so hard, and which wouldn't be so lonely?'

'I'd like to,' said Aunt Polly, with a sigh, 'but who would buy a place like this, half ruined and in such a wind-swept, desolate spot? And I should never be able to get your uncle to move. He loves this place, he loves this whole coast, and knows more about it than anyone else in the world. Well, well – it's no good wishing this and that. We must just go on until you and Dinah are old enough to earn your living.'

'Then I shall make a home for Mother, and she and Dinah and I will live together happily,' thought Philip, as he followed his aunt downstairs to fetch the old mattress. He called to Jack, and the two boys, with much puffing and panting, got the awkward mattress up the narrow stairway. Kiki encouraged them with shrieks and squawks. Joe, the handyman, frowned at the noise. He seemed to think Kiki was directing her screeches at him, and, when she found that her noises annoyed him, she did her best to make him jump by unexpected squawks in his ear.

Joe was taking up a small table and Jack's trunk. He set them down in the tower-room and looked out of the window. He seemed very bad-tempered, Philip thought. Not that he was good-tempered at any time – but he looked even sulkier than usual.

'What's up, Joe?' said Philip, who was not in the least afraid of the sullen man. 'Seeing things?'

The children had laughed over Joe's idea that there were 'things' wandering about at night. Joe frowned.

'Miss Polly shouldn't use this room,' he said. 'No, that she shouldn't, and I've told her so. It's a bad room. And you can see the Isle of Gloom from it too, when the mists lift – and it's bad to look on the Isle of Gloom.'

'Don't be silly, Joe,' said Philip, laughing.

'Don't be silly, Joe,' repeated Kiki, in an exact imitation of Philip's voice. Joe scowled at both boy and bird.

'Well, you take my word, Master Philip, and don't you go looking at the Isle of Gloom more than you can help. This is the only room you can see it from, and that's why it's a bad room. No good ever came from the Isle of Gloom. Bad men lived there, and bad deeds were done there, and wickedness came from the isle as long as anyone remembers.'

With this very weird warning the man departed down the stairs, his eyes angry, as he gazed back at the two boys with a scowl.

'Pleasant fellow, isn't he?' said Philip, as he and Jack unrolled the mattress. 'Half mad, I think. He must be daft to stay on here and do the work he does. He could get much more money anywhere else.'

'What's this Isle of Gloom he talks about?' said Jack, going to the window. 'What a weird name! I can't see any island, Tufty.'

'You hardly ever can see it,' said Philip. 'It lies right out there, to the west, and there is a reef of rocks round it over which waves continually break, flinging up spray. It seems always to have a mist hanging over it. No one lives there, though people used to, years and years ago.'

'I'd like to go there,' said Jack. 'There must be hundreds of birds on that island – quite tame and friendly. It would be marvellous to see them.'

'Tame and friendly. What do you mean, Freckles?' said Philip, in surprise. 'Look at the birds here – afraid even of Kiki!'

'Ah, but the birds on the Isle of Gloom would not have known man at all,' said Jack. 'They would not have learnt to be wary or cautious. I could get some simply marvellous photographs. Gosh, I'd like to go there!'

'Well, you can't,' said Philip. 'I've never been myself, and no one has, as far as I know. Look – will this be the best place for the mattress? We don't want it too near the window because the rain would wet it – and it often rains here.'

'Put it where you like,' said Jack, lost in dreams about the misty island and its unknown birds. He might see birds there that he had never seen at all – he might find rare nests and eggs. He might take the most wonderful bird-photographs in the world. Jack was quite determined to go to the Isle of Gloom if he could, in spite of all Joe's frightening tales.

'Come on down to the others,' said Philip at last, putting the rest of their clothes into the chest. 'I can't say you've been much help, Jack. Come on, Kiki.'

They went down the narrow, winding stair to find the others. It was good to think of the weeks ahead, with no work, no lessons – just bathing, climbing, rowing. They certainly would have fun!

6

The Days Go By

The girls had decided to have the two rooms. They were such small rooms, and it would be easier to keep two rooms tidier than one, if two people were to have them.

'There would never be room for anything if we tried to keep all our things in one room,' said Dinah, and Lucy-Ann agreed. She had been up to see the tower-room and liked it very much. She would have liked a room without glass panes too. It was almost as good as sleeping out-of-doors, thought the little girl, as she leaned out of one of the windows, and felt the sea-breeze streaming through her hair.

The girls' two rooms looked out over the sea, but in a different direction from the boys'. The Isle of Gloom could never be seen from there. Jack told Lucy-Ann what Joe had said, and Lucy-Ann looked rather alarmed.

'You needn't worry. Joe's full of strange beliefs and strange stories,' said Philip with a laugh. 'There's nothing in his stories, really – I believe he just likes frightening people.'

It was strange to sleep for the first time at Craggy-Tops. Lucy-Ann lay awake for a long time, listening to the muffled roar of the waves breaking on the rocks below. She heard the wind whistling too, and liked it. How different it all was from the quiet little town Uncle Geoffrey lived in! There everything seemed half dead – but here there was noise and movement, the taste of salt on her lips, the feel of the wind through her hair. It was exciting. Anything might happen at lonely Craggy-Tops.

Jack lay awake in the tower-room too. Philip was asleep on the mattress beside him. Jack got up and went to the window. The room was full of the wind, sweeping in at the sea-windows. Jack put his head out, and looked down.

There was a little moon rushing through the clouds. Down below was the swirling water, for the tide was in, beating over the black rocks. Spray flew up on the wind, and Jack felt sure he could feel a little on his cheek, high though his room was. He licked his lips. They tasted deliciously salty.

A bird cried in the night. It sounded sad and mournful, but Jack liked it. What bird was it? One he didn't know? The sea pounded away below and the wind swept up in gusts. Jack shivered. It was summer time, but Craggy-Tops was built in such a wind-driven spot that there were always draughts blowing around.

Then he jumped violently, for something touched his shoulder. His heart thumped, and then he laughed. It was only Kiki.

Kiki always slept with Jack, wherever he was. Usually she sat on the rail at the head of his bed, her big head tucked under her wing, but there was no rail this time, only a flat mattress laid on the floor.

So Kiki had found an uncomfortable perch on the edge of the chest – but when she heard Jack at the window she had flown to her usual perch, on his shoulder, making him jump violently. She nestled against him.

'Go to bed, naughty boy,' she said. 'Go to bed.'

Jack grinned. It was funny when Kiki by chance hit on the right sentences. He scratched her poll, talking in a low voice to her, so as not to wake Philip.

'I'll rig you up a perch of some sort tomorrow, Kiki,' he said. 'You can't sleep properly on the edge of that chest, I know. Now I'm going to bed. It's a wild night, isn't it? But I like it.'

He went back to bed, cold and shivering. But he soon got warm, cuddled up against Philip's back, and fell asleep, to dream of thousands of sea-birds walking tamely up to be photographed.

Life at Craggy-Tops was strange to Jack and Lucy-Ann at first, after all the years they had spent in an ordinary little house in an ordinary little town.

There was no electric light. There was no hot or cold water coming out of taps. There were no shops round the corner. There was no garden.

There were oil lamps to clean and trim each day, and candles to be put into candlesticks. There was water to be pumped up from a deep, deep well. Jack was interested in the well.

There was a small yard behind the house, backing on to the rocky cliff, and in it was the well that gave the household their water. Jack and Lucy-Ann were surprised that the water was not salty.

'No, it's pure drinking water all right,' said Dinah, lifting a heavy bucket from the chain. 'The well goes right down in the rocks, far below the sea-bed, to pure water, crystal clear and icy cold. Taste it.'

It was good to drink – as good as any iced water the children had drunk on hot summer days. Jack peered down the dark, deep well.

'I'd like to go down in that bucket and find out how deep the well-bottom is,' he said.

'You'd feel funny if you got stuck and couldn't get up again,' said Dinah, with a giggle. 'Come on, help me, Jack. Don't stand dreaming there. You're always dreaming.'

'And you're always so quick and impatient,' said Philip, nearby. Dinah gave him an angry look. She flared up very quickly, and it was easy to provoke her.

'Well, if you had to do as much as Lucy-Ann and

I have been told to do, you'd be a bit quicker too,' she snapped back. 'Come on, Lucy-Ann. Let's leave the boys to get on with their jobs. Boys aren't much good, anyway.'

'Yes, you'd better go, before I slap you,' yelled Philip after her, and then darted away before the angry Dinah could come after him. Lucy-Ann was puzzled and rather shocked at their continual quarrels, but she soon saw that they were over as quickly as they arose, and got used to them.

Shopping was quite a business. It meant that Joe had to get out the old car, and go off with a long list to the nearest village twice a week. If anything was forgotten, it had to be done without till the next visit. Vegetables were got from a small allotment that Joe worked at himself, in a sheltered dip of the cliff away behind the house.

'Let's go with Joe and have a ride in the car,' suggested Lucy-Ann one morning. But Philip shook his head.

'No good,' he said. 'We've asked Joe heaps of times, but he won't take us. He just refuses, and says he'll push us out of the car if we get in it to go with him. I did get in once, and he kept his word and pushed me out.'

'The old beast!' said Jack, astonished. 'I wonder you put up with him.'

'Well, who else would come here and work for us in this desolate place?' said Dinah. 'Nobody else. Joe wouldn't either if he wasn't so strange.'

Still, Lucy-Ann did ask Joe if she could go with him when he went shopping.

'No,' snapped the man, and scowled.

'Please, Joe,' said Lucy-Ann, looking at him pleadingly. Usually she got her own way when she badly wanted it – but not with Joe.

'I said no,' repeated the man, and walked off, his powerful arms swinging by his sides. Lucy-Ann stared after him. How horrid he was! Why wouldn't he take any of them in the car when he went shopping? Just bad temper, she supposed.

It was fun being at Craggy-Tops, in spite of so many things being difficult. Hot baths, for instance, could only be had once a week. At least, they *could* be taken every day, if someone lighted the copper fire, and was willing to carry pails of hot water down miles of stone passages to the one and only bath, set in a small room called the bathroom.

After doing this once, Jack decided that he didn't really care whether he had any more hot baths or not whilst he was at Craggy-Tops. He'd bathe in the sea two or three times a day, and make that do instead.

The girls were given household tasks to do, and did them as best they could. Aunt Polly did the cooking. Uncle Jocelyn did not appear even for meals. Aunt Polly took them to him in his study, and the children hardly remembered he was in the house.

The boys had to get in the water from the well, bring the wood in for the kitchen fire, and fill the burners in the oil stove with oil. They took it in turns with the girls to clean and trim the lamps. Nobody liked doing that, it was such a messy job.

Joe looked after the car and the allotment, did rough scrubbing, cleaned the windows when they became clogged up with salty spray, and did all kinds of other jobs. He had a boat of his own, a sound and good one with a small sail.

'Would he let us use it?' asked Jack.

'Of course not,' said Philip scornfully. 'And you'd better not try, without permission. He'd beat you if

you did. That boat is the apple of his eye. We are not allowed to set foot in it.'

Jack went to have a look at it. It was a very good boat indeed, and must have cost a lot of money. It had recently been painted and was in first-class order. There were oars, mast and sail, and a good deal of fishing tackle. Jack would dearly have loved to go out in it.

But even as he stood looking at it, wondering if he dared to put his foot into it and feel the boat rocking gently beneath him, the handyman appeared, his usual scowl even deeper.

'What are you doing?' he demanded, his eyes roving, so the whites showed plainly. 'That's *my* boat.'

'All right, all right,' said Jack impatiently. 'Can't I look at it?'

'No,' said Joe and scowled again.

'Naughty boy,' said Kiki, and screeched at Joe, who looked as if he would like to wring the bird's neck.

'Well, you certainly are a pleasant fellow,' said

Jack, stepping away from the boat, feeling suddenly afraid of the unfriendly man. 'But let me tell you this – I'm going out in a boat, *somehow*, and you can't stop me.'

Joe looked after Jack with eyes half closed and his mouth turned in angrily. That interfering boy! Joe would certainly stop him doing anything if he could!

7

An Odd Discovery

If it had not been for Joe, life at Craggy-Tops, once the children had settled down to their daily tasks, would have been very pleasant. There seemed so much to do that was fun – swimming in the sheltered cove, where the water was calm, was simply lovely. Exploring the damp dark caves in the cliffs was fun. Fishing from the rocks with a line was also very exciting, because quite big fish could be caught that way.

But Joe seemed to spoil everything, with his scowls and continued interference. He always seemed to appear wherever the children were. If they bathed, his sour face appeared round the rocks. If they fished, he came scowling out on the rocks and told them they were wasting their time.

'Oh, leave us alone, Joe,' said Philip impatiently. 'You act as if you were our keeper! For goodness' sake leave us to do what we want to do. We're not doing any harm.'

'Miss Polly said to me to keep an eye on you all,' said Joe sulkily. 'She said to me not to let you get into danger, see.'

'No, I don't see,' said Philip crossly. 'All I can see is that you keep popping up wherever we are and spoiling things for us. Don't keep prying on us. We don't like it.'

Lucy-Ann giggled. She thought it was brave of Philip to talk to the big man like that. He certainly was a nuisance. What fun they would have had if he had been jolly and good-tempered! They could have gone fishing and sailing in his boat. They could have fished properly with him. They could have gone out in the car and picnicked.

'But all because he's so sour and bad-tempered we can't do any of those things,' said Lucy-Ann. 'Why, we might even have tried to sail out to the Isle of Gloom to see if there were many birds there, as Jack so badly wants to do, if only Joe had been nice.'

'Well, he's not nice, and we'll never go to Gloom, and if we did get there, I bet there wouldn't be any birds on such a desolate place,' said Philip. 'Come on – let's explore that big cave we found yesterday.'

It really was fun exploring the caves on the shore. Some of them ran very far back into the cliff. Others had holes in the roofs, that led to upper caves. Philip said that in olden times men had used the caves for hiding in, or for storing smuggled goods. But there was nothing to be seen in them now except seaweed and empty shells.

'I wish we had a good torch,' said Jack, as his candle was blown out for the sixth time that morning. 'I shall soon have no candles left. If only there was a shop round the corner where we could slip along and buy a torch! I asked Joe to get me one when he went shopping in the car, but he wouldn't.'

'Oooh – here's a most enormous starfish!' said Philip, holding his candle down to the floor of the damp cave. 'Do look – it's a giant one, I'm sure.'

Dinah gave a shriek. She hated creepy-crawly things as much as Philip liked them. 'Don't touch it, and don't bring it near me.'

But Philip was a tease, and he picked up the great starfish, with its long five fingers, and walked over to Dinah with it. She flew into a furious rage.

'You beast! I told you not to bring it near me. I'll kill it if you do.'

'You can't kill starfish,' said Philip. 'If you cut one in half it grows new fingers, and, hey presto, it is two starfishes instead of one. So there! Have a look at it, Dinah – smell it – feel it.'

Philip pushed the great clammy thing near to his sister's face. Really alarmed, Dinah hit out, and gave Philip such a push that he reeled, overbalanced and fell headlong to the floor of the cave. His candle went out. There was a shout from Philip, then a curious slithering noise – and silence.

'Hi, Tufty! Are you all right?' called Jack, and held his candle high. To his enormous astonishment, Philip had completely disappeared. There was the starfish on the seaweedy ground – but no Philip was beside it.

The three children stared in the greatest

amazement at clumps of seaweed hanging from the walls of the cave, spreading over the ground. Wherever had Philip gone?

Dinah was scared. She had certainly meant to give Philip a hard blow – but she hadn't meant him to disappear off the face of the earth. She gave a yell.

'Philip! Are you hiding? Come out, idiot!'

A muffled voice came from somewhere. 'Hi! – where am I?'

'That's Tufty's voice,' said Jack. 'But where is he? He's nowhere in this cave.'

The children put their three candles together and looked round the small, low-roofed, seaweedy cave. It smelt very dank and musty. Philip's voice came again from somewhere, sounding rather frightened.

'I say! Where am I?'

Jack advanced cautiously over the slippery seaweed to where Philip had fallen when Dinah had struck him. Then suddenly he seemed to lose his footing, and, to the surprise of the watching girls, he too disappeared, seeming to sink down into the floor of the seaweedy cave.

By the wavering light of their two candles the girls tried to see what had happened to Jack. Then they saw the explanation of the mystery. The fronds of seaweed hid an opening in the floor of the cave, and when the boys had put their weight on to the seaweed covering the hole, they had slipped between the fronds down into some cave below. How strange!

'That's where they went,' said Dinah, pointing to a dark space between the seaweed covering that part of the floor. 'I hope they haven't broken their legs. However shall we get them out?'

Jack had fallen on top of poor Philip, almost squashing him. Kiki, left behind in the cave above, let out an ear-piercing screech. She hated these dark caves, but always came with Jack. Now he had suddenly gone, and the parrot was alarmed.

'Shut up, Kiki,' said Dinah, jumping in fright at the screech. 'Look, Lucy-Ann, there's a hole in the cave floor there, just between that thick seaweed. Walk carefully, or you'll disappear too. Hold up my candle as well as your own and I'll see if I can make out exactly what has happened.'

What had happened was really quite simple. First Philip had gone down the hole into a cave below, and then Jack had fallen on top of him. Philip was feeling frightened and bruised. He clutched Jack and wouldn't let go.

'What's happened?' he said.

'Hole in the cave floor,' said Jack, putting out his hands and feeling round to see how big the cave was they had fallen into. He touched rocky walls on each side of him at once. 'I say – this is a mighty small cave. Hi, girls, put the candles over the hole so that we can see something.'

A lighted candle now appeared above the boys and they were able to see a little.

'We're not in a cave. We're in a passage,' said Jack, astonished. 'At least, we're at the beginning of a passage. I wonder where it goes to . . . right into the cliff, I suppose.'

'Hand us down a candle,' called Philip, feeling better now. 'Oh, goodness – here's Kiki.'

'Can't you shut the door?' said Kiki, in a sharp voice, sitting hard on Jack's shoulder, glad to be with her master again. She began to whistle, and then told herself not to.

'Shut up, Kiki,' said Jack. 'Look, Philip – there really *is* a passage leading up there – awfully dark and narrow. And what a smell there is! Dinah, pass that candle down quickly, do!'

Dinah at last managed to hand down a lighted candle. She lay flat on the seaweedy cave floor, and just managed to pass the candle down through the hole. Jack held it up. The dark passage looked mysterious and strange.

'What about exploring it?' said Philip, feeling excited. 'It looks as if it ought to go below Craggy-Tops itself. It's a secret passage.'

'More likely a short crack in the cliff rocks that leads nowhere at all,' said Jack. 'Kiki, don't peck my ear so hard. We'll go into the open air soon. Hi, you girls! We think we'll go up this funny passage. Are you coming?'

'No, thanks,' said Lucy-Ann at once, who didn't at all like the sound of a seaweedy passage that ran, dark and narrow, through the cliffs. 'We'll stay here till you come back. Don't be long. We've only got one candle now. Have you some matches in case your candle goes out?'

'Yes,' said Jack, feeling in his pocket. 'Well, goodbye for the present. Don't fall down the hole.'

The boys left the dark hole under which they stood and began to make their way up the damp passage. The girls could no longer hear their voices or footsteps. They waited patiently in the cave above, lighted by one flickering candle. It was cold and they shivered, glad of their warm jerseys.

The boys were a very long time. The two girls became impatient and then alarmed. What could have happened to them? They peered down the hole between the great fronds of seaweed and listened. Not a sound could be heard.

'Oh dear – do you think we ought to go after them?' said Lucy-Ann desperately. She would be frightened to death going up that dark secret passage, she was sure, and yet if Jack was in need of help she would have no hesitation in jumping down and following him.

'Better go and tell Joe and get him to come and help,' said Dinah. 'He'd better bring a rope, I should think. The boys would never be able to climb up through the hole back into this cave without help.'

'No, don't let's tell Joe,' said Lucy-Ann, who disliked the man thoroughly, and was afraid of him. 'We'll wait a bit longer. Maybe the passage was a very long one.'

It was – far longer than the boys expected. It twisted and turned as it went through the cliff, going upwards all the time. It was pitch-dark, and the candle did not seem to light it very much. The boys bumped their heads against the roof every now and again, for it was sometimes only shoulder-high.

It grew drier as it went up. Soon there was no seaweedy smell at all, but the air felt stale and musty. It was rather difficult to breathe.

'I believe the air is bad here,' panted Philip, as they went on. 'I can hardly breathe. Once or twice I thought our candle was going out, Freckles. That would mean the air was very bad. Surely we shall come to the end of this passage soon.'

As he spoke, the passage went steeply upwards and was cut into rough steps. It ended abruptly in a rocky wall. The boys were puzzled.

'It's not a real passage, then,' said Philip, disappointed. 'Just a crack in the cliff rocks, as you said. But these do look like rough steps, don't they?'

The light of the candle shone down on to the

steps. Yes – someone had hewn out those steps at one time – but why?

Jack held the candle above his head – and gave a shout.

'Look! Isn't that a trap-door above our heads? That's where the passage led to – that trap-door! I say – let's get it open if we can.'

Sure enough, there was an old wooden trap-door, closing the exit of the passage, above their heads. If only they could lift it! Wherever would they find themselves?

8

In the Cellars

'Let's push at it together,' said Philip, in excitement. 'I'll put the candle down on this ledge.'

He stuck the candle firmly into a crack on the ledge. Then he and Jack pushed hard at the trap-door just above their heads. A shower of dust fell down, and Philip blinked his eyes, half blinded. Jack had closed his.

'Blow!' said Philip, rubbing his eyes. 'Come on, let's try again. I felt it move.'

They tried again, and this time the trap-door suddenly gave way. It lifted a few inches, and then fell back again, setting free another cloud of dust.

'Get a rock or big stone and we'll stand on it,' said Jack, red with excitement. 'A bit more of a push and we'll get the thing right open.'

They found three or four flattish stones, put them in a stout pile, and stood on them. They pushed against the trap-door, and to their delight it lifted right up, and fell backwards with a thud on the floor above, leaving a square opening above the heads of the boys.

'Give me a heave up, Jack,' said Philip. He got such a shove that he shot out through the trap-door opening and landed on a rocky floor above. It was dark there and he could see nothing.

'Hand up the candle, Freckles, and then I'll haul you up,' said Philip. The candle was handed up, but went out suddenly.

'Blow!' said Philip. 'Oh glory, what's that?'

'Kiki, I expect,' said Jack. 'She's flown up.'

Kiki had not made a sound or said a word all through the secret passage. She had been alarmed at the dark strange place, and had clung hard to Jack all the way.

Philip hauled Jack up, and then groped in his pocket for the matches to light the candle again. 'Where do you suppose we are?' he said. 'I simply can't imagine.'

'Feels like the other end of the world,' said Jack.

'Ah – that's better, now we can see.'

He held up the lighted candle and the two boys looked round.

'*I* know where we are,' said Philip suddenly. 'In one of the cellars at Craggy-Tops. Look – there are boxes of stores over there. Tins of food and stuff.'

'So there are,' said Jack. 'My word, what a fine store your aunt keeps down here! Golly, this is quite an adventure. Do you suppose your aunt and uncle know about the secret passage?'

'I shouldn't think so,' said Philip. 'Aunt Polly would be sure to have mentioned it to us, I should think. I don't seem to know this part of the cellars very well. Let me see – where is the cellar door now?'

The boys wandered down the cellar, trying to find the way out. They came to a stout wooden door, but, to their surprise, it was locked.

'Blow!' said Philip, annoyed. 'Now we shall have to creep all the way back down that passage again. I don't feel like doing that, somehow. Anyway, this isn't the door that leads out of the cellars into the kitchen. You have to go up steps to that one. This must be a door that shuts off one part of the cellars from the other. I don't remember seeing it before.'

'Listen – isn't that somebody coming?' said Jack suddenly, his sharp ears hearing footsteps.

'Yes – it's Joe,' said Philip, hearing the familiar cough he knew so well. 'Let's hide. I'm not going to tell Joe about that passage. We'll keep it to ourselves. Shut the trap-door down quickly, Jack, and then we'll hide behind this archway here. We could slip out quietly when Joe opens the door. Blow out the candle.'

They shut the trap-door quietly and then, in the pitch darkness, hid behind the stone archway near the door. They heard Joe putting a key into the lock. The door swung open, and the man appeared, looking huge in the flickering light of his lantern. He left the door open, and went towards the back of the cellar, where the stores lay.

The boys had on rubber shoes, and could have slipped out without Joe knowing anything at all – but Kiki chose that moment to imitate Joe's hollow

cough. It filled the cellar with mournful echoes, and Joe dropped his lantern with a crash. The glass splintered and the light went out. Joe gave a howl of terror and fled out of the door at once, not even pausing to lock it. He brushed against the two boys as he went, and gave another screech of fright, feeling their warm bodies as he passed.

Kiki, thrilled at the result of her coughing

imitation, gave an unearthly screech that sent Joe headlong through the other part of the cellar, up the steps and through the cellar door. He almost fell as he appeared in the kitchen, and Aunt Polly jumped in astonishment.

'What's the matter? What has happened?'

'There's things down there!' panted Joe, his face looking as scared as it ever could look.

'Things! What do you mean?' said Aunt Polly severely.

'Things that screech and yell and clutch at me,' said Joe, sinking into a chair, and closing his eyes till nothing but the thinnest slits could be seen.

'Nonsense!' said Aunt Polly, stirring a saucepan vigorously. 'I don't know why you wanted to go down there anyway. We don't need anything from the cellars this morning. I've plenty of potatoes up here. Pull yourself together, Joe. You'll frighten the children if you behave like this.'

The two boys had collapsed into helpless laughter when they had seen poor Joe running in alarm from the cellar, yelling for all he was worth. They clutched each other and laughed till they ached. 'Well, Joe is always trying to frighten us by tales of peculiar "things" that wander about at night,' said Jack, 'and now he's been caught by his own silly stories – and been almost frightened out of his wits.'

'I say – he's left the key in the door,' said Philip, who had now lighted his candle again. 'Let's take it. Then, if ever we want to use that passage again, we can always get out this way if we want to, by unlocking the door.'

He put the big key into his pocket, grinning. Maybe the jumpy man would think one of the 'things' he was always talking about had gone off with his key.

The boys went into the part of the cellar they knew. Philip looked with interest at the door through which they had come.

'I never knew there was another cellar beyond this first one,' he said, looking round the vast underground room. 'How did I never notice that door before, I wonder?'

'Those boxes must have been piled in front of

it to hide it,' said Jack. There were empty boxes by the door, and now that he thought of it, Philip had remembered seeing them in a big pile every time he had gone into the cellar. They had been neatly piled in front of that door. A trick of Joe's, no doubt, to stop the children going into the second cellar, where all those stores were kept. How silly and childish! Well, he couldn't stop them going there now.

'We can go there through the secret passage, or we could go there through the door, because I've got the key now,' thought Philip, pleased at the idea of being able to outwit the man if he wanted to.

'I suppose those steps lead up to the kitchen, don't they?' said Jack, pointing to them. 'Is it safe to go up, do you think? We don't want anyone to see us, or they'd ask awkward questions.'

'I'll slip up to the top, open the door a crack, and listen to see if anyone is about,' said Philip. So up he went. But Joe had gone out and his aunt was no longer there, so the big kitchen was empty and silent. The boys were able to slip out, go to the outer door, and run down the cliff path without anyone seeing them at all.

'The girls will wonder whatever had become of us,' said Jack, suddenly remembering Dinah and Lucy-Ann, waiting patiently for them in the cave where the hole was that led into the passage. 'Come on – let's give them a surprise, shall we? They'll be expecting us to come back through the secret passage – they'll never expect us to come back this way.'

They made their way down to the rocky shore. They went to the caves they had explored that morning and found the one that had the hole. The two girls were sitting by the hole, anxiously discussing what they ought to do.

'We really *must* go and get help now,' said Lucy-Ann. 'I'm sure something has happened to the boys. Really I am.'

Philip suddenly spotted the giant starfish again, the one that had caused all the trouble. Very silently he picked it up. Without making a sound, he crept over the seaweedy cave floor to poor Dinah.

He placed the starfish on her bare arm, where it slithered down in a horrible manner.

Dinah leapt up with a shriek that was even worse than Kiki's loudest one. 'Oh – oh Philip's back again, the beast! Wait till I get hold of you, Philip! I'll pull all your hair out of your head! You hateful boy!'

In one of her furious rages Dinah leapt at Philip, who ran out of the caves and on to the sandy shore in glee. Lucy-Ann threw her arms round Jack. She had been very anxious about him.

'Jack! Oh, Jack, what happened to you? I waited so long. How did you come back this way? Where did the passage lead to?'

Shrieks and yells and shouts from Dinah and Philip made it impossible for Jack to answer, especially as Kiki now joined in the row, screeching like an express train in a tunnel.

There was a fine fight going on between Philip and Dinah. The angry girl had caught her brother, and was hitting out at him for all she was worth.

'I'll teach you to throw starfish at me. You mean

pig! You know I hate those things. I'll pull all your hair out.'

Philip got free and ran off, leaving a few of his hairs in Dinah's fingers. Dinah turned a furious face to the others.

'He's a beast. I shan't talk to him for days. I wish he wasn't my brother.'

'It was only a bit of fun,' began Jack, but this made matters worse. Dinah flew into a temper with him too, and looked so fierce that Lucy-Ann was quite alarmed, and thought she would have to defend Jack if Dinah rushed to slap him.

'I won't have anything to do with any of you,' stormed Dinah, and walked off angrily.

'Now she won't hear all we've found this morning,' said Jack. 'What a spitfire she is! Well, we'll have to tell *you*, Lucy-Ann. We've had a real adventure.'

Dinah, walking off in a fury, suddenly remembered that she had not heard the story of the secret passage and where it came out. Forgetting her rage, she turned back at once.

She saw Lucy-Ann and the two boys together.

Philip turned his back on her as she came up. But Dinah could be as sudden in her good tempers as she was in her bad ones. She put her arm on Philip's.

'Sorry, Philip,' she said. 'What happened to you and Jack in that secret passage? I'm longing to know.'

So peace was restored again, and soon the two girls were listening in the greatest excitement to all that the boys had to tell.

'It was an adventure, I can tell you,' said Jack. So it was – and there were more to come!

9

A Strange Boat

The girls would not go up the secret passage, no matter how much the boys urged them to. They shuddered to think of the dark, narrow, winding tunnel, and although they agreed that it was very exciting, they did not want to feel the thrill of creeping along it by themselves.

'I suppose Dinah's afraid of giant starfish jumping out at her, or something,' said Philip in disgust. 'And Lucy-Ann takes her side.'

But even teasing would not make the girls try the passage, though they never tired of hearing about it. The boys slipped down into the cellar the next day, and found that Joe had once again piled up the boxes in front of the second door, so that it was quite hidden. It was puzzling, but he often did silly spiteful things. Anyway, they had the key of the door. That was something.

The weather became fine and hot. The sun shone down out of a cloudless sky and the children went about in bathing-suits. They were soon burnt as brown as toast. Philip, Dinah and Lucy-Ann spent more time than Jack in the water. The boy was quite mad over the wild birds that infested the coast in such numbers. He was forever identifying terns and skuas, cormorants, gulls and others. He did not want Lucy-Ann with him, much to her dismay.

'The birds are learning to know me,' he explained to his sister. 'But they don't know you, Lucy-Ann.

You keep with the others, there's a good girl. Anyway, we can't both leave Tufty and Dinah, it would be rude.'

So for once Lucy-Ann was not Jack's shadow, and spent most of her time with the others. But she usually knew where Jack was, and, when it was about time for him to return, she would always watch for him.

Dinah thought she was silly. She would never have dreamt of watching for Philip. 'I'm only too glad when he gets out of the way,' she said to Lucy-Ann. 'Horrid tease! He nearly made me go mad last year when he put earwigs under my pillow, and they all crawled out in the middle of the night.'

Lucy-Ann thought that sounded horrid. But by now she was used to Philip and his peculiar ways. Even when he was only wearing swimming trunks he seemed able to secrete some kind of creature about his body. Yesterday it had been a couple of friendly crabs. But when he had accidentally sat down on one, and it had nipped him, he had come to the conclusion that crabs were better in the sea than out of it.

'Anyway, I'm glad Freckles takes Kiki with him when he goes bird-watching,' said Dinah. 'I quite like Kiki, but now that she has taken to imitating all the birds around here, it is rather sickening. I'm surprised Aunt Polly puts up with her as well as she does.'

Aunt Polly had become fond of the parrot. It was an artful bird and knew that it had only to murmur 'Poor dear Polly' to get anything it liked out of Aunt Polly. Joe had been well and truly ticked off by Aunt Polly the day he had gone shopping in the car and had forgotten the parrot's sunflower seeds. The children had been delighted to hear the man so well scolded.

Uncle Jocelyn's experience of Kiki was definitely not so good. One hot afternoon the parrot had flown silently in at the open window of the study, where Uncle Jocelyn sat, as usual, bent double over his old papers and books. Kiki flew to the book-shelf and perched there, looking round her with interest.

'How many times have I told you not to whistle?' she said in a stern voice.

Uncle Jocelyn, lost in his books, came out of them with a start. He had never seen the parrot and had forgotten that one had come to the house. He sat puzzling his head to know where such an extraordinary speech came from.

Kiki said nothing more for a time. Uncle Jocelyn came to the conclusion that he had been mistaken, and he dropped his head to study his papers once more.

'Where's your handkerchief?' asked Kiki sternly.

Uncle Jocelyn felt sure that his wife was somewhere in the room, for Kiki imitated Aunt Polly's voice very well. He groped in his pocket for a handkerchief.

'Good boy,' said the parrot. 'Don't forget to wipe your feet now.'

'They're not dirty, Polly,' said Uncle Jocelyn in surprise, thinking that he was speaking to his wife. He was puzzled and annoyed. Aunt Polly did not usually come and disturb him like this by giving him unnecessary orders. He turned round to tell her to go, but could not see her.

Kiki gave a hollow cough, exactly like Joe's. Uncle Jocelyn, now certain that the man was also in the room, felt most irritable. Why must everyone walk in and disturb him today? Really, it was unbearable.

'Get out,' he said, thinking that he was speaking to Joe. 'I'm busy.'

'Oh, you naughty boy,' said the parrot, in a reproving tone. Then it coughed again, and gave a realistic sneeze. Then, for a while, there was complete silence.

Uncle Jocelyn settled down again, forgetting all about the interruption at once. Kiki did not like being ignored like that. She flew from the bookshelf on to Uncle Jocelyn's grey head, giving one of her railway-engine screams as she did so.

Poor Uncle Jocelyn leapt to his feet, clutched at his head, dislodged Kiki, and gave a yell that brought Aunt Polly into the room at once. Kiki sailed out of the window, making a cackling sound that sounded just like laughter.

'What's the matter, Jocelyn?' asked Aunt Polly, alarmed.

Uncle Jocelyn was in a rage. 'People have been in and out of this room all the morning, telling me to wipe my feet and not to whistle, and somebody threw something at my head,' he fumed.

'Oh – that was only Kiki,' said Aunt Polly, beginning to smile.

'Only Kiki! And who on earth is Kiki?' shouted Uncle Jocelyn, furious at seeing his wife smile at his troubles instead of sympathising with them.

'The parrot,' said Aunt Polly. 'The boy's parrot, you know.'

Uncle Jocelyn had forgotten all about Jack and Lucy-Ann. He stared at his wife as if she had gone mad.

'What boy – and what parrot?' he demanded. 'Have you gone crazy, Polly?'

'Oh dear,' sighed Aunt Polly. 'How you do forget things, Jocelyn!' She reminded him of the two children who had come for the holidays, and explained about Kiki. 'She's the cleverest parrot you ever saw,' said Aunt Polly, who had now completely lost her heart to Kiki.

'Well,' said Uncle Jocelyn grimly, 'all I can say is that if that parrot is as clever as you think it is, it will keep out of my way – because I shall throw all my paperweights at it if it comes in here again.'

Aunt Polly, thinking of her husband's very bad aim whenever he threw anything, gave a glance at the window. She thought she had better keep it closed, or she might find everything in the room smashed by paperweights one day. Dear, dear, what annoying things did happen, to be sure! If it wasn't children clamouring for more to eat, it was Joe worrying her; and if it wasn't Joe, it was the parrot; and if it wasn't the parrot, it was Uncle Jocelyn threatening to throw his paperweights about. Aunt Polly closed the window firmly, went out of the room, and shut the door sharply.

'Don't slam the door,' came Kiki's voice from the passage. 'And how many times have I . . .'

But for once Aunt Polly had no kind word for Kiki. 'You're a bad bird,' she said sternly to the parrot. 'A very bad bird.'

Kiki sailed down the passage with an indignant screech. She would find Jack. Jack was always good and kind to her. Where was Jack?

Jack was not with the others. He had gone with his field-glasses to the top of the cliff, and was lying on his back, looking with pleasure at the birds soaring above his head. Kiki landed on his middle and made him jump.

'Oh – it's you, Kiki. Be careful with your claws, for goodness' sake. I've only got my bathing-suit on. Now keep quiet, or you'll frighten away the birds. I've already seen five different kinds of gulls today.'

Jack got tired of lying on his back at last. He sat up, pushed Kiki off his middle, and blinked round. He put his field-glasses to his eyes again, and looked out over the sea in the direction of the Isle of Gloom. He had not seen it properly yet.

But today, though most of the distant hills behind him were lost in the heat haze, for some reason or other the island could be quite plainly seen, jutting up from the sea to the west. 'Gosh!' said Jack, in surprise, 'there's that mystery island that Joe says is a bad island. How clearly it can be seen today! I can see hills jutting up – and I can even see the waves dashing spray over the rocks that go round it!'

Jack could not see any birds on the island, for his glasses were not strong enough to show him anything more than the island itself and its hills. But the boy felt certain that it was full of birds.

'Rare birds,' he said to himself. 'Birds that people don't know any more. Birds that might nest there undisturbed year after year, and be as tame as cats. Golly, I wish I could go there. What a tiresome nuisance Joe is not to let us use his boat! We could get to the island in it quite easily if the sea was as calm as it is today. Blow Joe!'

The boy swept his glasses around the jagged coast, and then stared hard in surprise at something. It couldn't be somebody rowing a boat along the coast, about a mile or so away. Surely it couldn't. Joe had said that nobody but himself had a boat for miles and miles – and Aunt Polly had said that nobody lived anywhere near Craggy-Tops at all –

not nearer than six or seven miles, anyway.

'And yet there's someone in a boat out there on the sea to the west of this cliff,' said Jack, puzzled. 'Who is it? I suppose it *must* be Joe.'

The man in the boat was too far away to make out. It might be Joe and it might not. Jack came to the conclusion that it must be. He glanced at the sun. It was pretty high, so it must be dinner-time. He'd go back, and on the way he would look and see if Joe's boat was tied up in the usual place. If it was gone, then the man in the boat must be Joe.

But the boat was not gone. It was in its usual place, firmly tied to its post, rocking gently in the little harbour near the house. And there was Joe too, collecting driftwood from the beach for the kitchen fire. Then there *must* be someone else not far away who had a boat of his own.

Jack ran to tell the others. They were surprised and pleased. 'We'll go and find out who he is, and pal up with him, and maybe he'll take us out fishing in the boat,' said Philip at once. 'Good for you, Freckles. Your old field-glasses have found out something besides birds for you.'

'We'll go and see him tomorrow,' said Jack. 'What I really want is a chance to go out to the Isle of Gloom and see if there are any rare birds there. I just feel I *must* go there! I really have got a sort of hunch about it.'

'We won't tell Joe we've seen someone else with a boat,' said Dinah. 'He'd only try to stop us. He hates us doing anything we like.'

So nothing was said to Joe or to Aunt Polly about the stranger in the boat. The next day they would find him and talk to him.

But something was to happen before the next day came.

10

Night Adventure

That night Jack could not sleep. The moon was full and shone in at his window. The moonlight fell on his face and he lay there, staring at the big silvery moon, thinking of the gulls he had seen gliding and circling on the wind, and the big black cormorants that stood on the rocks, their beaks wide open as they digested the fish they had caught.

He remembered the Isle of Gloom, as he had seen it that morning. It looked mysterious and exciting – so far away, and lonely and desolate. Yet people had lived there once. Why did no one live there now? Was it so desolate that no one could make a living there? What was it like?

'I wonder if I could possibly see it tonight, in the light of the full moon,' thought Jack. He slipped off the mattress without waking Philip, and went to the window. He stared out.

The sea was silvery bright in the moonlight. Where rocks cast shadows, deep black patches lay on the sea. The waters were calmer than usual, and the wind had dropped. Only a murmur came up to Jack as he stood at the window.

Then he stared in surprise. A sailing boat was coming over the water. It was still a good way out, but it was making for the shore. Whose boat was it? Jack strained his eyes but could not make it out. A sailing boat making for Craggy-Tops in the middle of the night! It was odd.

'I'll wake Tufty,' he thought, and went to the mattress. 'Tufty! Philip! Wake up and come to the window.'

In half a minute Philip was wide awake, leaning out of the narrow window with Jack. He too saw the sailing boat, and gave a low whistle that awoke Kiki and brought her to Jack's shoulder in surprise.

'Is it Joe in the boat?' wondered Philip. 'I can't tell if it's his boat or not from here. Anyway, let's get down to the shore and watch it come in, Freckles. Come on. I'm surprised that he should be out at night, when he's always telling us about "things" that wander around the cliff in the dark – but it probably isn't him.'

They put on shorts and jerseys, and their rubber shoes, and made their way down the spiral stair. They were soon climbing down the steep cliff path. Under the moon the sailing boat came steadily in, the night wind behind it.

'It *is* Joe's boat,' said Philip at last. 'We can see it plainly now. And there's Joe in it. He's alone, but he's got a cargo of some sort.'

'Maybe he's been fishing,' said Jack. 'Let's give him a fright, Philip.'

The boys crept up to where the boat was heading. Joe was furling the sail. Then he began to row to the shore, towards the little harbour where he always tied up his boat. The boys crouched down behind a rock. Joe brought the big boat safely in, and then tied the rope to the post. He turned to pull out whatever cargo he had – and at that very moment the boys jumped out at him, giving Red Indian whoops and rocking the boat violently.

The man was taken unawares, lost his balance and fell into the water, going overboard with a terrific splash. He came up at once, his face gleaming in the moonlight. The boys did not like the expression on it. Joe climbed out of the water, shook himself like a dog, and came towards the boys determinedly.

'Golly – he's going to lick us,' said Jack to Philip. 'Come on – we must run for it.'

But the way to the house was barred by the big powerful body of the angry man.

'Now I'll show you what happens to boys who come spying around at night,' he said between his teeth. Jack tried to dodge by, but Joe caught hold of him. He swung his big fist into the air and Jack gave a yell. At the same moment Philip charged Joe full in the middle, and the winded man gasped for breath, and let go of Jack. The boys sped off over the beach at once, heading away from the steep cliff path that led to the house. Joe was after them immediately.

'The tide's coming in,' gasped Jack, as he felt water running over his ankles. 'We must turn back.

We'll be caught by the tide and pounded against the rocks.'

'We can't turn back.We shall be licked black and blue by Joe,' panted Philip. 'Jack – make for that cave. We can perhaps creep up that secret passage. We simply must. I really don't know what he mightn't do if he was in a rage. He might even kill us.'

Quite terrified now, the boys floundered into the cave, the waves running round their ankles. Joe came splashing behind them. Ah – he had got those boys now! Wait till he had done with them! They wouldn't leave their beds again at night!

The boys found the hole in the floor of the cave they were looking for and disappeared down it into the darkness of the secret passage. They heard Joe breathing heavily outside in the upper cave. They hoped and prayed he would not slip down the hole too.

He didn't. He stood outside by the entrance, waiting for the boys to come out. He had no idea there was a secret passage there. He stood, panting heavily, clenching his fist hard. A big wave covered his knees. Joe muttered something. The tide was coming in rapidly. If those boys didn't come out immediately they would be trapped there for the night.

Another wave ran up, almost as high as the angry man's waist. It was such a powerful wave that he at once left the cave entrance and tried to make his way back across the beach. He could not risk being dashed to pieces against the cliff by the incoming tide.

'Those boys can spend the night in the caves, and I'll deal with them tomorrow morning early,' thought Joe grimly. 'As soon as the tide goes down in the morning I'll be there – and they'll be mighty sorry for themselves when I've finished with them.'

But the boys were not shivering inside the cave. They were once more climbing up the secret passage, this time in complete darkness. The passage was terrifying enough – but not nearly so alarming as Joe.

They came at last to the trap-door and pushed

it open. They clambered out on to the rocky cellar floor, and shut the trap-door.

'Take my hand,' said Jack, shivering as much with cold as with fright. 'We'll make our way towards the door as best we can. Come on. You know the direction, don't you? I don't.'

Philip thought he did, but he found that he didn't. It took the boys some time to find the cellar door. They felt all round the rocky walls of the cellar, and at long last, after falling over boxes of all kinds, they came to the door. It was not locked. Thank goodness they had taken away the key. Philip pushed at the door and it opened.

The pile of boxes on the other side fell over with a terrific crash that echoed all round the cellar. The boys stood listening to see if anyone would hear and come. But nobody did. They piled up the boxes again as best they could and crept up the cellar steps and into the moonlit kitchen.

They wondered where Joe was. Was he still waiting for them at the entrance to the caves?

He was not. He had made fast his boat, removed

several things from it, and then had climbed the cliff path to the house. He had gone to his bedroom, just off the kitchen, gloating over the thought of the two boys shivering in the caves, when a terrific noise came to his ears.

It was the pile of boxes overturning down in the cellar, but Joe did not know that. He stood in his bedroom, rooted to the ground. What was that noise? He did not dare to go and find out. If he had, he would have seen two figures stealing through the moonlit kitchen towards the hall. He would have seen them scurrying up the stairs as quietly as mice.

Soon the boys were on their mattress, glad to be there safe and sound. They chuckled when they thought of Joe waiting in vain for them. And, down in his bedroom, Joe chuckled to think of how he would wait outside the cave the next morning, armed with a rope, and give those two boys a good hiding.

They all fell asleep at last.

Joe was up first, piling driftwood on the kitchen fire. He did his jobs, and then tied the rope-end round his waist. It was time he went down to the beach and caught those boys. The tide would soon be down low enough for them to come out.

Then he stopped still in the greatest astonishment – for into the kitchen, as bold as brass, came all four children, chattering away loudly.

'What's for breakfast? Golly, I'm hungry.'

'Did you have a good night, boys? We did.'

'Fine. We must have slept all the night through.' These words were from Philip. Jack joined in, delighted to see amazement and wonder appear on Joe's face. 'Yes, we slept like logs. Even if Kiki had done her imitation of a railway express, I don't think we'd have woken up.'

'What's for breakfast, Joe?' asked Dinah. Both the girls knew about the boys' adventure the night before, and were entering into the fun of teasing Joe. He evidently still thought the boys were down in the caves.

'You two boys been asleep in your room all night?' asked Joe at last, hardly able to believe his eyes and ears.

'Where else should we sleep?' said Philip impudently. 'On the Isle of Gloom?'

Joe turned away, puzzled and taken aback. It couldn't have been these two boys last night. It was true he had not seen their faces clearly, but he had felt certain they were Philip and Jack. But now that was plainly impossible. No one could have got out of those caves at high tide – and yet here were the boys. It was disturbing and puzzling. Joe didn't like it.

'I'll go down to those caves now and watch to see who comes out,' he thought at last. 'Then I'll know who it was spying on me last night.'

So down he went – but though he watched for two hours, nobody came from the caves. Which was not very surprising, because there was nobody there.

'He just simply can't understand it,' said Jack, grinning, as he watched the tall man from the cliff path. 'What a good thing we didn't tell anyone about the secret passage! It came in mighty useful last night.'

'He'll think you and Philip were two of the "things" he's always trying to frighten us with,' said Dinah. 'Silly old Joe! He must think we are babies to be frightened of anything *he* would say.'

'What are we going to do today when we've finished our jobs?' asked Lucy-Ann, polishing the lamp she had been cleaning. 'It's such a fine day. Can't we go for a picnic – walk over the cliff and along the coast?'

'Oh yes – and we'll see if we can find that man I saw in a boat yesterday,' said Jack, remembering. 'That would be fine. Maybe he'll let us go in his boat. Dinah, ask your Aunt Polly if we can take our dinner with us.'

Aunt Polly said yes, and in about half an hour they set off, passing Joe on the way. He was now working on his allotment, over the edge of the cliff, behind the house.

'Did you have a good night, Joe?' yelled Philip. 'Did you sleep all night long, like a good boy?'

The man scowled and made a threatening noise.

Kiki imitated him, and he bent down to pick up a stone to throw at her.

'Naughty boy!' screeched Kiki, flying high into the air. 'Naughty, naughty boy! Go to bed at once, naughty boy!'

11

Bill Smugs

'Whereabouts did you see the strange boat, Freckles?' asked Philip, as they went over the cliffs.

'Over there, beyond those rocks that jut out,' said Jack, pointing. 'Quite a big boat, really. I wonder where it's kept when it's not in use. Somebody must live fairly near it – but I couldn't see any houses.'

'There aren't any proper houses near,' said Philip. 'People used to live about here ages ago, but there was fighting and burning, and now there are only ruined places. But there might be a tumbledown shack of some sort, all right for a man who wants a lonely kind of holiday.'

They walked on over the cliffs, Kiki sailing up into the air every now and again to join a surprised gull, and making noises exactly like the sea-birds, but more piercing.

Philip collected a large and unusual caterpillar

from a bush, much to Dinah's dismay, and put a lizard into his pocket. After that Dinah walked a good distance from him, and even Lucy-Ann was a bit wary. Lucy-Ann did not mind live creatures as Dinah did, but she wasn't particularly anxious to be asked to carry lizards or caterpillars, as she might quite well be requested to do if Philip decided to take home some other creature that, if put in his pocket, might eat the caterpillar or lizard already there!

They all walked on happily, enjoying the rough sea-breeze, the salty smell of the sea, and the sound of the waves against the rocks below. The grass was springy beneath their feet, and the air was full of gliding birds. This was a lovely holiday, lovely, lovely!

They came to a jutting part of the cliff and walked out almost to the edge. 'I can't see signs of any boat on the water at all,' said Jack.

'You're sure you didn't imagine it?' said Philip. 'It's funny there's not a thing to be seen today – a boat is not an easy thing to hide.'

'There's a sort of cove down there,' said Lucy-Ann, pointing to where the cliff turned in a little, and there was a small beach of shining sand. 'Let's go down and picnic there, shall we? We can bathe first. It's awfully windy up here; I can hardly get my breath to talk.'

They began to climb down the steep and rocky cliff. The boys went first and the girls followed, slipping a little now and again. But they were all good climbers, and reached the bottom of the cliff in safety.

Here it was sheltered from the rushing wind and was warm and quiet. The children slipped off their jerseys and shorts and went into the water to bathe. Philip, who was a good swimmer, swam right out to some black rocks that stuck out from the water, high and forbidding. He reached them, and climbed up to rest for a while.

And then he suddenly saw a boat, on the other side of the rocks! There was a flat stretch there, and on it, pulled up out of reach of the waves, was the boat that Jack had seen on the sea the day before.

No one could possibly see the boat unless he, like Philip, was on those particular rocks, for, from the shore, the high rocks hid the flat stretch facing seawards, where the boat lay.

'Whew!' whistled Philip in surprise. He got up and went over to the boat. It was a fine boat with a sail, and was almost as big as Joe's. It was called *The Albatross*. There were two pairs of oars in it.

'Well!' said Philip. 'What a strange place to keep a boat – right out here on these rocks! Whoever owns it would have to swim out whenever he wanted to get it. Funny!'

He shouted to the others. 'The boat's here – on these rocks. Come and see it.'

Soon all the children were examining the boat. 'That's the one I saw,' said Jack. 'But where's the owner? There's no sign of him anywhere.'

'We'll have our lunch and then we'll have a good look-see,' said Philip. 'Come on – back to the shore we'll go. Then we'll separate after our picnic and hunt round properly for the man who owns this boat.'

They swam back to the shore, took off their wet

things, set them out to dry in the sun, and put on their dry clothes. Then they sat down to enjoy the sandwiches, chocolate and fruit that Aunt Polly had prepared for them. They lolled in the sun, tired with their swim, hungry and thirsty, enjoying the food immensely.

'Food's gorgeous when you're really hungry,' said Lucy-Ann, taking a huge bite at her sandwich.

'I always am hungry,' said Jack. 'Shut up, Kiki – that's the best part of my apple you've pecked. I've got some sunflower seeds for you in my pocket. Can't you wait?'

'What a pity, what a pity!' said Kiki, imitating Aunt Polly when something went wrong. 'What a pity, what a pity, what a . . .'

'Oh, stop her,' said Dinah, who knew that the parrot was quite capable of repeating a brand-new sentence a hundred times without stopping. 'Here, Kiki – have a bite of my apple, do.'

That stopped Kiki, and she ran her beak into the apple in delight, pecking out a bit that kept her busy for some time.

A quarrel nearly blew up between Dinah and Philip over the large caterpillar which made its way out of the boy's pocket, over the sand, towards Dinah. She gave a shriek, and was about to hurl a large shell at Philip when Jack picked up the caterpillar and put it back into Philip's pocket.

'No harm done, Dinah,' he said. 'Keep your hair on! Don't let's start a free fight now. Let's have a peaceful day.'

They finished up every crumb of the lunch. 'The gulls won't get much,' said Philip lazily, shaking out the papers, then folding them up and putting them into his pocket. 'Look at that young gull – it's as tame as anything.'

'I wish I had my camera here,' said Jack longingly, watching the enormous young gull walking very near. 'I could get a marvellous snap of him. I haven't taken any bird pictures yet. I really must. I'll find my camera tomorrow.'

'Come on,' said Dinah, jumping up. 'If we're going to do a spot of man-hunting, we'd better begin. I bet I find the strange boatman first.'

They separated, Jack and Philip going one way and the girls going the other. They walked on the sandy little beach, keeping close to the rocky cliffs. The girls found that they could not get very far, because steep rocks barred their way after a bit, and they had to turn back.

But the boys managed to get past the piece of cliff that jutted out and sheltered the little cove they had been picnicking in. On the other side of the cliff was another cove, with no beach at all, merely flattish rocks that shelved upwards to the cliff. The boys clambered over these rocks, examining the creatures in the pools as they went. Philip added a sea snail to the collection in his pocket.

'There's a break in the cliff just over there,' said Jack. 'Let's explore it.'

They made their way towards the gap in the cliff. It was much wider than they expected when they got there. A stream trickled over the rocks towards the sea, running down from somewhere halfway up the cliff.

'Must be spring water,' said Jack, and tasted it.

'Yes, it is. Hallo – look, Tufty!'

Philip looked to where Jack pointed, and saw floating in a pool a cigarette end, almost falling to pieces.

'Someone's been here, and quite recently too,' said Jack, 'else the tide would have carried that cigarette end away. This is exciting.'

With the cigarette end as a proof of someone's nearness, the boys went on more eagerly still. They came to the wide crack in the cliff – and there, a little way up, built close against the rocky slope, was a tumbledown hut. The back of it was made of the cliff itself. The roof had been roughly mended. The walls were falling to pieces here and there, and, in winter, it would have been quite impossible to live in it. But someone was certainly living there now, for outside, spread over a stunted bush, was a shirt set out to dry.

'Look,' said Jack, in a whisper. 'That's where our boatman lives. What a lovely hidey-hole he's found!'

The boys went quietly up to the tumbledown hut. It was very, very old, and had probably once

belonged to a lonely fisherman. A whistling came
from inside the hut.

'Do we knock at the door?' said Philip, with a

nervous giggle. But at that moment someone came out of the open doorway and caught sight of the boys. He stood gaping in great surprise.

The boys stared back without a word. They rather liked the look of the stranger. He wore shorts and a rough shirt, open at the neck. He had a red, jolly face, twinkling eyes, and a head that was bald on the top, but had plenty of hair round the sides. He was tall and strong-looking, and his chin jutted out below his clean-shaven mouth.

'Hallo,' he said. 'Coming visiting? How nice!'

'I saw you out in your boat yesterday,' said Jack. 'So we came to see if we could find you.'

'Very friendly of you,' said the man. 'Who are you?'

'We're from Craggy-Tops, the house about a mile and a half away,' said Philip. 'I don't expect you know it.'

'Yes, I do,' said the man unexpectedly. 'But I thought only grown-ups lived there – a man and a woman – and an odd-job man.'

'Well, usually only grown-ups *do* live there,' said

Philip. 'But in the hols my sister and I come there too, to stay with our Aunt Polly and Uncle Jocelyn. And these hols two friends of ours came as well. This is one of them – Jack Trent. His sister Lucy-Ann is somewhere about. I'm Philip Mannering and my sister is Dinah – she's with Lucy-Ann.'

'I'm Bill Smugs,' said the man, smiling at all this sudden information. 'And I live here alone.'

'Have you just suddenly come here?' asked Jack, in curiosity.

'Quite suddenly,' said the man. 'Just an idea of mine, you know.'

'Not much to come for here,' said Philip. 'Why did you come?'

The man hesitated for a moment. 'Well,' he said, 'I'm a bird-watcher. Interested in birds, you know. And there are a great many unusual birds here.'

'Oh!' cried Jack, in the greatest delight. 'Do you like birds too? I'm mad on them. Always have been. I've seen crowds here that I've only seen in books before.'

And then the boy plunged into a list of the

unusual birds he had seen, making Philip yawn. Bill Smugs listened, but did not say very much. He seemed amused at Jack's enthusiasm.

'What particular bird did you hope to see here, Mr Smugs?' asked Jack, stopping at last.

Bill Smugs seemed to consider. 'Well,' he said, 'I rather hoped I might see a Great Auk.'

Jack looked at him in astonished silence that changed to awe. 'The Great Auk!' he said, in a voice mixed with surprise and wonder. 'But – but isn't it extinct? Surely there are no Great Auks left now? Golly – did you really think you might see one?'

'You never know,' said Bill Smugs. 'There might be one or two left somewhere – and think what a scoop it would be to discover them!'

Jack went brick-red with excitement. He looked out over the sea towards the west, where the Isle of Gloom lay hidden in a haze.

'I bet you thought there might be a chance of them on a desolate island like that,' he said, pointing to the west. 'You know – the Isle of Gloom. You've heard about it, I expect.'

'Yes, I have,' said Bill Smugs. 'I certainly have. I'd like to go there. But it's impossible, I believe.'

'Would you take us out in your boat sometimes?' asked Philip. 'Joe, the odd-job man, has a fine boat, but he won't let us use it, and we'd love to go fishing sometimes, and sailing too. Do you think it's awful cheek to ask you? But I expect you find it a bit lonely here, don't you?'

'Sometimes,' said Bill Smugs. 'Yes, we'll go fishing and sailing together – you and your sisters too. It would be fun. We'll see how near we can go to the Isle of Gloom too, shall we?'

The boys were thrilled. At last they could sail a boat. They went off to call the girls.

'Hi, Dinah! Hi, Lucy-Ann!' yelled Jack. 'Come and be introduced to our new friend – Bill Smugs!'

12

A Treat – and a Surprise for Joe

Bill Smugs proved to be a fine friend. He was a jolly fellow, always ready for a joke, patient with Kiki, and even more patient with Philip's ever-changing collection of strange pets. He did not even say anything when Philip's latest possession, an extra large spider, ran up the leg of his shorts. He merely put his hand up, took hold of the wriggling spider, and deposited it on Philip's knee.

Dinah, of course, was nearly in hysterics, but mercifully the spider decided that captivity was boring, ran into a rock crevice and disappeared.

The children visited Bill Smugs nearly every day. They went fishing in his boat and brought home marvellous catches that made Joe's mouth fall open in amazement. Bill showed them how to sail the boat too, and soon the four children could manage it perfectly well themselves. It was great fun sailing about in a good strong breeze.

'Almost as fast as a motor boat,' said Philip in glee. 'Bill, I *am* glad we found you.'

To Jack's disappointment Bill Smugs did not seem to want to talk endlessly about birds, nor did he want to go off with Jack and watch the birds on the cliffs or on the sea. He was quite willing to listen to Jack raving about birds, though, and produced many fine new bird books for him, which he said Jack could keep for himself.

'But they're new,' protested Jack. 'Look, the pages of this one haven't even been cut – you've not read them yourself, sir. You read them first.'

'No, you can have them,' said Bill Smugs, lighting his cigarette. 'There's a bit about the Great Auk in one of them. I'm afraid we shall never find that bird after all. No one has seen it for about a hundred years.'

'It *might* be on the Isle of Gloom – or on some equally deserted, desolate island,' said Jack hopefully. 'I do wish we could go there and see. I bet there would be thousands of frightfully tame birds there, sir.'

This eternal talk about birds always bored Dinah. She changed the subject.

'You should have seen Joe's face when we brought in our catch of fish yesterday,' she said, with a grin. 'He said, "You never caught those from the rocks. You've been out in a boat".'

'You didn't tell him you had?' said Bill Smugs at once. Dinah shook her head.

'No,' she said. 'He'd try to spoil our pleasure if he knew we used your boat.'

'Do your uncle and aunt know you've met me?' asked Bill. Dinah shook her head again.

'Why?' she asked. 'Don't you want them to know? What does it matter whether they do or not?'

'Well,' said Bill Smugs, scratching the bald top of his head. 'I came here to be alone – and to watch the birds – and I don't want people coming round spoiling things for me. I don't mind you children, of course. You're fun.'

Bill Smugs lived all alone in the tumbledown hut. He had a comfortable car, which he kept under a tarpaulin at the top of the cliff, in as sheltered a place as possible. He went into the nearest town to do his shopping whenever he wanted to. He had brought a mattress and other things to the hut, to make it as comfortable as he could.

The children were thrilled when they knew he had a car as well as a boat. They begged him to take them out in it next time he went.

'I want to buy a torch,' said Jack. 'You remember that secret passage we told you about, Bill? Well, it's difficult to go up it carrying a candle – a torch would be much handier. I could buy one if you'd take me in your car.'

'I'd like one too,' said Philip. 'And, Jack – you said you wanted some camera film, because you'd left yours behind at Mr Roy's. You can't take photographs of birds unless we get some. You could get that too.'

The girls wanted things as well, so Bill Smugs agreed to take them the next day. They all crowded into the car in excitement the following morning.

'Joe's going into the town as well today,' said Dinah, with a giggle. 'It would be funny if we saw him, wouldn't it? He *would* get a surprise.'

Bill Smugs' car was really a beauty. The boys, who knew about cars, examined it in delight.

'It's new,' said Jack. 'This year's, and a jolly fast one. Bill, are you very rich? This car must have cost a lot of money. You must be awfully well-off.'

'Not very,' said Bill, with a grin. 'Now – off we go.'

And off they went, cruising very swiftly, once they left the bad coast road behind. The car was well-sprung, and seemed to surge along.

'Golly, isn't it different from Aunt Polly's old car!' said Dinah, enjoying herself. 'It won't take us any time to get to the town.'

They were very soon there. Bill Smugs parked the car, and then went off by himself, after arranging with the children to meet them for lunch at a very grand hotel.

'I wonder where he's gone,' said Jack, staring after him. 'We might just as well have kept all together. I wanted to go to that stuffed animal shop with him, and see some of the stuffed birds there.'

'Well, you could see he didn't want us,' said Dinah, who was disappointed too. She was very fond of Bill Smugs now and had saved up some money to buy him an ice cream. 'I expect he has got business of his own to do.'

'What is his business?' asked Lucy-Ann. 'He must do something besides bird-watching, I should think. Not that he does much of that, now that he knows us.'

'He never said what his work was,' said Jack. 'Anyway, why should he? He's not like us, always wanting to blurt out everything. Grown-ups are different. Come on – let's find a shop that sells torches.'

They found one that had extremely nice pocket torches, small and neat. The beam was strong, and the boys could well imagine how the dark secret passage would be lighted up, once they turned on their torches. They each bought a torch.

'Now we needn't light our bedroom candles at night,' said Dinah. 'We can use torches.'

They went to buy rolls of film to fit Jack's camera. They bought sweets and biscuits, and a small bottle of strong-smelling scent for Aunt Polly.

'Now we'd better get some sunflower seeds for Kiki,' said Jack. Kiki gave a squawk. She was on Jack's shoulder as usual, behaving very well for once. Every passer-by stared at her in surprise, of course, and the parrot enjoyed this very much. But, except for sternly telling a surprised errand-boy to stop whistling at once, Kiki hardly said a word. She was pleased with the sunflower seeds, which she adored, and gobbled up a few in the shop.

The children looked in the shops for a time, waiting for one o'clock to come, so that they might join Bill Smugs at the hotel. And then, quite suddenly, they saw Joe.

He was coming along the street in the old car, hooting at a woman crossing the road. The children clutched one another, wondering if he would see them, half hoping that he would.

And he did. He caught sight of Philip first, then saw Jack with Kiki on his shoulder, and then the two girls behind. He was so overcome with amazement that he let the car swerve across the road, almost knocking down a policeman.

'Here, you! What do you think you're doing?' yelled the policeman angrily. Joe muttered an apology, and then looked for the children again.

'Don't run away,' said Jack to the others. 'He can't chase us in the car. Just walk along and take no notice of him.'

So they walked down the street, talking together, pretending not to see Joe and taking no notice at all of his shouts.

Joe simply could not believe his eyes. How did the children get here? There was no bus, no train, no coach they could take. They had no bicycles. It

was too far for them to have walked there in the
time. Then how was it they were here?

The man hurried to park his car, meaning to go after the children and question them. He parked it and jumped out. He chased after the four children, but at that moment they reached the very grand hotel where they had arranged to meet Bill Smugs, and ran up the steps.

Joe did not dare to follow the children into the grand hotel. He stood at the bottom of the big flight of steps, looking after them in annoyed surprise. It was astonishing enough to find them in the town – but even more astonishing to find them disappearing into the most expensive hotel in the place.

Joe sat down at the bottom of the steps. He meant to wait till they came out. Then he would pack them into his car and take them home, and tell Miss Polly where he'd found them. She wouldn't be best pleased to hear they were wasting hard-earned money at expensive hotels, when they could easily take a packet of sandwiches with them.

The children giggled as they ran up the steps. Bill Smugs was waiting for them in the lounge. He showed them where to wash and comb their hair.

They all met together again in a few minutes and went into the restaurant to have lunch.

It was a magnificent lunch. The children ate everything put in front of them, and finished up with the biggest ice creams they had ever seen.

'Oh, Bill, that was grand,' said Dinah, sinking back into her comfortable chair with a sigh. 'Simply marvellous. A real treat. Thanks awfully.'

'I think you must be a millionaire,' said Lucy-Ann, watching Bill count out notes to the waiter in payment of the bill. 'Golly, I've eaten so much that I feel I really can't get up and walk.'

Jack remembered Joe, and wondered if the man was watching for them. He got up to see.

He peeped out of a window that looked on to the hotel's main entrance. He saw Joe sitting patiently down at the bottom of the steps. Jack went back to the others, grinning.

'Is there a back entrance to this hotel?' he asked Bill Smugs. Bill looked surprised.

'Yes,' he said. 'Why?'

'Because Joe is sitting outside the hotel entrance

waiting for us,' said Jack. Bill nodded, understanding.

'Well, we'll depart quietly by the back entrance,' he said. 'Come on. It's time we went, anyway. Got all you wanted from the shops?'

'Yes,' said the children, and trooped out after him. He led them to the back of the hotel, and out of a door there into a quiet street. He took them to where he had parked his car, and they all got in, happy at having had such a lovely day.

They sped back to the coast, and got out of the car at the nearest point to Craggy-Tops. They hurried over the cliff, eager to get back before Joe did.

He did not arrive until about an hour later, looking dour and grim. He put away the car and went to the house. The first thing he saw was the group of four children playing down on the rocks. He stood and stared in angry astonishment.

There was a mystery somewhere. And Joe meant to find out what it was. He wasn't going to be puzzled and defeated by four children. Not he!

13

Joe Is Tricked Again

Joe thought about the mystery of the children being in the town, with, as far as he knew, no possible way of getting there – except by walking, and this they had not had time to do. He came to the conclusion that they must know someone who gave them a lift there.

So he set himself to watch the children closely. He managed to find jobs that always took him near them. If they went down to the shore, he would be there, collecting driftwood. If they stayed in the house, he stayed too. If they went up on the cliff, Joe followed. It was most annoying for the children.

'He'll follow us and find out about Bill Smugs and his boat and car,' said Lucy-Ann. 'We haven't been able to go and see him at all today – and if he goes on like this we shan't be able to go tomorrow either.'

It was impossible to give Joe the slip. He was very clever at keeping a watch on the children, and soon they grew angry. The two girls went up into the tower-room with the boys that night and discussed the matter together.

'*I* know,' said Jack suddenly. 'I know how we can give him the slip properly, and puzzle him terribly.'

'How?' asked the others.

'Why, we'll all go into the caves,' said Jack. 'And we'll slip down the hole into the secret passage, and go up to Craggy-Tops cellar, slip out of there whilst Joe is waiting down on the beach for us, and go over the cliffs to Bill.'

'Oooh, that *is* a good idea,' said Philip. The girls were doubtful about it, for they neither of them liked the idea of the secret passage very much. Still – they all had torches now, and it would be a good chance to use them.

So next day, with Joe close on their heels, the four children and Kiki went down to the beach.

'Joe, for goodness' sake leave us alone,' said Philip. 'We're going into the caves, and no harm

can come to us there. Go away!'

'Miss Polly said I was to keep an eye on you,' repeated Joe. He had told the children this times without number, but they knew it wasn't the real reason. Joe enjoyed making himself a nuisance. He wanted to poke his nose into everything they did.

They went into the caves. Joe wandered outside, putting driftwood into his sack. The children all slipped down the hole that led to the secret passage, and then, with their torches switched on, they made their way along it.

The girls didn't like it at all. They hated the smell, and when they found that in one part it was difficult to breathe, they stopped.

'Well, it's no good going back,' said Philip, giving Dinah a shove to make her go on. 'We've come more than halfway now. Do go on, Dinah. You're holding us up.'

'Don't push!' said Dinah. 'I shall stop if I want to.'

'Oh, shut up arguing, you two,' groaned Jack. 'I believe you'd start a quarrel if you were in a ship that was just about to sink, or an aeroplane about to crash. Get on, Dinah, we'll be out soon.'

Dinah was about to start an argument with Jack too, when Kiki gave a mournful cough, so exactly like Joe's that the children at first thought the man must have found the passage, and all of them, Dinah as well, hurried forward at once.

'It's all right – it was only that wretch Kiki,' said Jack, relieved, as Kiki coughed again. They pushed on, and at last came to the end of the passage. They all stared at the trap-door above their heads, brightly lit by the light of their four torches.

Up it went, and over with a crash. The boys climbed up to the cellar floor and then helped the girls up. They shut the trap-door, went to the cellar door, which was shut, and pushed it open. The boxes on the other side fell over again with a familiar crashing noise.

The children went through the door, shut it, piled the boxes up again, and then went up the cellar steps to the big kitchen. No one was there. That was lucky.

Out they went, and up to the cliff. Keeping to the path, where they were well hidden from the shore below, they hurried off to find their friend Bill Smugs. They grinned to think of Joe waiting down on the beach for them to come out of the caves.

Bill Smugs was tinkering with his boat. He waved cheerily as they came up.

'Hallo,' he said, 'why didn't you come and see me yesterday? I missed you.'

'It was because of Joe,' said Jack. 'He keeps following us around like a shadow. I think he probably suspects we have a friend who has a car, and he means to find out who it is.'

'Well, don't tell him anything,' said Bill quickly.

'Keep things to yourself. I don't want him prying around here. He doesn't sound at all a nice person.'

'What are you doing to your boat?' asked Jack. 'Are you going out in it?'

'I thought I would,' said Bill. 'It's a fine day, the sea is fairly calm, yet there's a nice breeze – and I half thought I might sail near to the Isle of Gloom.'

There was an excited silence. The Isle of Gloom! All the children wanted to see it close to – and Jack badly wanted to land there. If only Bill would take them with him!

Jack looked out to the west. He could not see the island, for once again there was a low heat haze on the sea. But he knew exactly where it was. His heart beat fast. The Great Auk might be there. Anyway, even if it wasn't, all kinds of other sea-birds would be there – and probably as tame as anything. He could take his camera – he could . . .

'Bill – please, please take us with you!' begged Lucy-Ann. 'Oh, do! We'll be very good, and you know, now that you have taught us how to sail a boat, we can really help.'

'Well – I meant to take you,' said Bill, lighting a cigarette, and smiling round at the children. 'I wanted to go yesterday, and when you didn't come, I put the trip off till today. We'll go this afternoon, and take our tea with us. You'll have to give Joe the slip again. He mustn't see you sailing in my boat or he'd probably try to stop you.'

'Oh, Bill! We'll be along first thing this afternoon,' said Jack, his eyes gleaming very green.

'Thanks most *awfully*,' said Philip.

'Shall we really see the Isle of Gloom close to?' asked Lucy-Ann, in excitement.

'Can't we land there?' said Dinah.

'I don't think so,' said Bill. 'You see, there is a ring of dangerous rocks around it, and although there may once have been a passage somewhere through them, and possibly is now, for all I know, I don't know where it is. I'm not going to risk drowning you all.'

'Oh,' said the children, disappointed. They would have been quite willing to run the risk of being drowned, for the sake of trying to land on the bad isle.

'You'd better go back and have an early lunch, if your aunt will let you have it,' said Bill. 'I don't want to be too late in starting. The tide will help us, if we get off fairly early.'

'All right,' said the four, jumping up from the rocks at once. 'Goodbye till this afternoon, Bill. We'll bring tea with us – as nice as we can, to reward you for waiting for us.'

They set off home again, talking eagerly of the coming trip. Joe had said so many frightening things about the desolate island that the children couldn't help feeling excited at the idea of seeing it.

'I wonder if Joe is still on the beach, watching for us outside the caves,' said Jack. The children went cautiously to the edge of the cliff and peeped over. Yes – he was still down there. What a sell for him!

They went to Craggy-Tops and found Aunt Polly. 'Aunt, could we possibly have an early lunch, and then go off and take our tea with us?' asked Philip. 'Will it be any trouble? We'll help to get the lunch, and we don't mind what we have.'

'There's a cold pie in the larder,' said Aunt Polly considering. 'And some tomatoes. And there are some stewed plums. Dinah, you lay the table, and the others can set out the food. I'll make you some sandwiches for your tea, and there's a ginger cake you can have too. Lucy-Ann, can you put the kettle on to boil? You can have some tea in a thermos flask if you like.'

'Oh, thank you,' said the children, and set to work at once. They laid a place for Aunt Polly, but she shook her head.

'I don't feel very well today,' she said. 'I've got a bad headache. I shan't want anything. I shall have a good long rest while you are out this afternoon.'

The children were sorry. Certainly Aunt Polly did look tired out. Philip wondered if his mother had sent any more money to help things along a bit, or whether Aunt Polly was finding things very difficult. He didn't like to ask her in front of the others. Soon the children were having their dinner, and then, the tea being packed up and ready, they set off over the cliff.

They had not seen Joe. The man was still down on the beach, now feeling puzzled, and most annoyed with the vanished children. He felt certain they were in the caves. He went in himself and called to them.

There was no answer, of course. He called again and again. 'Well, if they've lost themselves in the caves, it will be good riddance of bad rubbish,' he said to himself. He decided to go up and report the matter to Miss Polly.

So up he went. The children had gone, and Aunt Polly was washing up. She glanced sharply at Joe.

'Where have you been all the morning?' she asked. 'I wanted you, and you were nowhere to be found.'

'Looking for them children,' said Joe. 'It's my belief they've gone into the caves down there, and got lost. I been calling and calling for them.'

'Don't be so silly, Joe,' said Aunt Polly. 'You're just making the children an excuse for your laziness. You know quite well they are not in the caves.'

'Miss Polly, I seed them go in, and I didn't seed them come out,' began Joe indignantly, 'I was on the beach all the time, wasn't I? Well, I tells you, Miss Polly, them children went into the caves, and they're there still.'

'No, they're not,' said Aunt Polly firmly. 'They have just gone off for a picnic. They came in, had an early lunch and went out again. So don't come to me any more with silly stories about them being lost in the caves.'

Joe's mouth dropped open. He simply could not believe his ears. Hadn't he been on the beach by the caves all the morning? He would have seen the children as soon as they came out.

'Don't pretend to be so surprised,' said Aunt Polly sharply. 'Just stir yourself and do a few jobs quickly. You will have to do this afternoon all the things you didn't do this morning. I expect the children did go into the caves – but they must have slipped out when you were not looking. Don't just stand there! Get on with some of your work.'

Joe shook himself, shut his mouth and went off

silently to do some jobs in the house. He was full of amazement. He remembered how one night he had chased two boys into the caves, thinking they were Philip and Jack – and the tide had come up and imprisoned them in the caves – but they were not there the next morning.

And now the four children had done the same thing. Joe thought it was decidedly uncanny. He didn't like it. Now those children had given him the slip again. Where had they gone? Well, it wasn't much good trying to find out that afternoon – not with Miss Polly in such a bad temper anyway!

14

A Glimpse of the Isle of Gloom

The children hurried over the cliffs to Bill Smugs and his boat. He was ready for them. He put their packet of sandwiches and cake, their thermos, and a packet of biscuits and chocolate of his own, into the boat. Then they all got in.

Bill had brought the boat to shore, instead of hiding it out by the rocks. He pushed off, wading in the water till the boat floated. Then in he jumped, and took the oars till they were away from the rocks.

'Now then,' he said, in a little while, when they were well beyond the rocks and out at sea. 'Now then, boys, up with that sail and let's see how you do it!'

The boys put up the sail easily. Then they took turns at the tiller, and Bill was pleased with them. 'You are good pupils,' he said approvingly. 'I believe you could take this boat out alone now.'

'Oh, Bill – would you let us?' asked Jack eagerly. 'You could trust us, really you could.'

'I might, one day,' said Bill. 'You would have to promise not to sail out very far, that's all.'

'Oh yes, we'd promise anything,' said the children earnestly. How thrilling it would be to set off in Bill's boat all by themselves!

There was a good wind and the boat sped along smoothly, rocking a little every now and again as she came to a swell. The sea was really very calm.

'It's lovely,' said Jack. 'I do like the flapping noise the sail makes – and the sound of the water slapping against the boat, and the steady whistling of the wind . . .'

Dinah and Lucy-Ann let their hands trail in the cool, silky water. Kiki watched with interest from her perch on the big sail. She could hardly keep her balance there, and had to half-spread her wings to help her. She seemed to be enjoying the trip as much as the children.

'Wipe your feet and shut the door,' she said

to Bill Smugs, catching his eye. 'How many times have I ...'

'Shut up, Kiki!' cried everyone at once. 'Don't be rude to Bill, or he'll throw you overboard.'

Kiki cackled with laughter, rose into the air and joined a couple of startled sea-gulls, announcing to them that they had better use their handkerchiefs. Then she gave an ear-piercing shriek that made the gulls sheer off in alarm. Kiki returned to her perch, pleased with herself. She did enjoy creating a sensation, whether it was among human beings, birds or animals.

'I still can't see the Isle of Gloom,' said Jack, who was keeping a sharp look-out for it. 'Whereabouts is it, Bill? I seem to have lost my sense of direction now I'm right out at sea.'

'Over there,' said Bill, pointing. The children followed his finger, but could see nothing. Still, it was exciting that the 'bad island', as Joe called it, was coming nearer and nearer.

The sailing boat sped on, and the wind freshened a little as they got further out. The girls' hair streamed out behind them, or blew all over their faces, and Bill gave an exclamation of annoyance as the wind neatly whipped his cigarette from his fingers and swept it away.

'Now, if Kiki was any use at all, she would fly after that and bring it back to me,' said Bill, cocking an eye at the parrot.

'Poor Kiki,' said the parrot, sorrowfully shaking her head. 'Poor old Kiki. What a pity, what a pity, what . . .'

Jack aimed an old shell at her and she stopped with a cackle of laughter. Bill tried to light another cigarette, which the wind made rather difficult.

After a while Jack gave a sudden cry. 'Look! Land ho! Isn't that the Isle of Gloom? It must be.'

They all looked hard. Looming up out of the heat haze was land, there was no doubt about it.

'Yes – that's the island all right,' said Bill, with great interest. 'It's fairly big too.'

The boat drew nearer. The island became clearer and the children could see how rocky and hilly it was. Round it was a continual turmoil of water. Surf and spray were flung high into the air, and here and there the children could see jagged rocks sticking up from the sea.

They went nearer in. The water was rough and choppy now, and Lucy-Ann began to look a little green. She was the only one who was not a first-rate sailor. But she bravely said nothing, and soon the seasick feeling began to pass off a little.

'Now you can see the wide ring of rocks running round the island,' said Bill Smugs. 'My word, aren't they wicked! I guess many a boat has been wrecked on them at some time or another. We'll cruise round a bit, and see if we can spot any entry. But – we don't go any nearer, so it's no use begging me to.'

The Albatross was now in a very choppy sea indeed and poor Lucy-Ann went green again. 'Have a dry biscuit, Lucy-Ann,' said Bill Smugs, noticing her looks. 'Nibble it. It may keep off that sick feeling.'

It did. Lucy-Ann nibbled the dry biscuit gratefully and was soon able to take an interest in the trip once more. The Isle of Gloom certainly lived up to

its name. It was a most desolate place, as far as the children could see. It seemed to be made of jagged rocks that rose into high hills in the middle of the island. A few stunted trees grew here and there, and grass showed green in some places. The rocks were a curious red colour on the seaweed side of the island, but black everywhere else.

'There are heaps and heaps of birds there, just as I thought,' said Jack, looking through his field-glasses in excitement. 'Golly – just look at them, Bill!'

But Bill would not leave the tiller. It was dangerous work cruising near to the ring of rocks in such a choppy sea. He nodded to Jack. 'I'll take your word for it,' he said. 'Tell me if you recognise any birds.'

Jack reeled off a list of names. 'Bill, there are thousands and thousands of birds!' he cried. 'Oh, do, do let's land on the island. Find a way through this ring of rocks somehow. Please, please do.'

'No,' said Bill firmly. 'I said not. It would be a dangerous business to get to the island even if we knew the way, and I don't. I'm not risking all our lives for the sake of seeing a few birds at close quarters – birds you can see at Craggy-Tops any day.'

The sailing boat went on its way round the island, keeping well outside the wicked ring of rocks over which waves broke continually, sending spray high into the air. The children watched them, and noticed how they raced over the treacherous rocks, making a roaring noise that never stopped. It was somehow very thrilling, and the children felt exultant and wanted to shout.

Jack could see the island most clearly because of his field-glasses. He kept them glued to his eyes, looking at the hundreds of birds, both flying and sitting, that he could see. Philip tapped his arm.

'Let someone else have a look too,' he said. 'Hand over the glasses.'

Jack didn't want to, because he was afraid of missing seeing a Great Auk, but he did at last give them to Philip. Philip was not so interested in the birds – he swept the coast of the island with the glasses – and then gave an exclamation.

'Hallo! There are still houses or something on the island. Surely people don't live there now.'

'Of course not,' said Bill Smugs. 'It's been deserted for ages. I can't imagine why anyone ever *did* live on it. They could not have farmed it or used it for fishing – it's a desolate, impossible sort of place.'

'I suppose what I can see are only ruins,' said Philip. 'They seem to be in the hills. I can't make them out really.'

'Anyone walking about – any of Joe's "things"?' asked Dinah, with a laugh.

'No, nobody at all,' said Philip. 'Have a look through the glasses, Dinah – and then Lucy-Ann. I don't wonder it's called the Isle of Gloom. It certainly is a terribly gloomy-looking place – nothing alive on it except the sea-birds.'

The girls had a turn of looking through the glasses too. They didn't like the look of the island at all. It was ugly and bare, and had an extraordinary air of forlornness about it.

The sailing boat went all round the island, keeping well outside the rocks that guarded it. The only place where there might conceivably be an entrance between the rocks was a spot to the west. Here the sea became less choppy, and although spray was flung up high, the children could see no rocks on the surface. The spray was flung by waves racing over rocks nearby.

'I bet that's the only entrance to the island,' said Jack.

'Well, we're not going to try it,' said Bill Smugs at once. 'I'm going to leave the island now, and head for calmer water. Then we'll take down the sail and have our tea, bobbing gently about instead of tossing and pitching like this. Poor Lucy-Ann keeps on turning green.'

Jack took a last look through his glasses – and gave such a shout that Dinah nearly over-balanced, and Kiki fell off her perch above.

'Whatever is it?' said Bill Smugs, startled.

'A Great Auk!' yelled Jack, the glasses glued to his eyes. 'It is, it is – an enormous bird – with small wings close to its sides – and a big razor-like bill. It's a Great Auk!'

Bill gave the tiller to Jack for a moment and took the glasses. But he could see no Great Auk, and he handed them back to the excited boy, whose green eyes were gleaming with joy.

'I expect it's one of the razorbills,' he said. 'The Great Auk is much like a big razorbill, you know – you've let your wish be father to the thought, old man. That wasn't a Great Auk, I'll be bound.'

But Jack was absolutely convinced that it was. He could not see it any longer, but, as they left the island behind, the boy sat looking longingly backwards at it. The Great Auk was there. He was sure it was. He was certain he had seen one. How could Bill suggest it was a razorbill?

'Bill – Bill – do go back,' begged Jack, hardly able to contain himself. 'I know it was an auk – a Great Auk. I suddenly saw it. Imagine it! What will the world say if they know I've found a Great Auk, a bird that's been extinct for years!'

'The world wouldn't care much,' said Bill Smugs

drily. 'Only a few people keen on birds would be excited. Calm yourself a bit – I'm afraid it certainly wasn't the bird you thought.'

Jack couldn't calm himself. He sat looking terribly excited, his eyes glowing, his face red, his hair blown about in the wind. Kiki felt the excitement and came down to his shoulder, pecking at his ear to get his attention.

'It was a Great Auk, it was, it was,' said Jack, and Lucy-Ann slipped a hand in his arm and squeezed it. She too was sure it was a Great Auk – and anyway she wasn't going to spoil her brother's pleasure by saying that it wasn't. Neither Philip nor Dinah believed that it was.

They had their tea on calmer water, with the sail down and the boat drifting where it pleased. Jack could eat nothing, though he drank his tea. Lucy-Ann, hungry now after her seasickness, ate Jack's share of the tea, and enjoyed it. The others enjoyed themselves too. It had been an exciting afternoon.

'Can we sail your boat by ourselves sometime,

as you promised?' asked Jack suddenly. Bill Smugs looked at him sharply.

'Only if you promise not to go very far out,' he said. 'No rushing off to find the Great Auk on the Isle of Gloom, you know.'

As this was the idea at the back of Jack's mind, the boy went red at once. 'All right,' he said at last. 'I promise not to go to the Isle of Gloom in your boat, Bill. But may we really go out by ourselves other days?'

'Yes, you may,' said Bill. 'I think you really know how to manage the boat all right – and you can't come to much harm if you choose a calm day.'

Jack looked pleased. A dreamy expression came over his face. He knew what he meant to do. He would keep his word to Bill Smugs – he would not go to the Isle of Gloom in Bill's boat – but he would go in someone else's. He would practise sailing and rowing in *Bill's* boat – and as soon as he was absolutely sure of handling it, he would borrow Joe's boat, and go to the island in that.

This was a bold and daring plan – but Jack was

so thrilled at the idea of finding a Great Auk, when everyone else thought it was extinct, that he was willing to run any risk to get to the island. He was sure he could find the entrance to the ring of rocks. He would furl the sail when he got near the rocks and do some rowing. Joe's boat was big and heavy, but Jack thought he could manage it well enough.

He said nothing to the others whilst Bill was there. Bill mustn't know. He was jolly and kind and a good friend – but he was a grown-up, and grown-ups always stopped children doing anything risky. So Jack sat in the rocking boat and thought out his daring plan, not hearing the others' remarks or teasing.

'He's gone off to the island to see his Great Auk,' said Dinah, with a laugh.

'Poor old Jack – that bird has quite taken his appetite away,' said Philip.

'Wake up!' said Bill, giving Jack a nudge. 'Be a little sociable.'

After tea they decided to row back, taking it in turns. Bill thought it would be good for them to have some exercise, and the children enjoyed handling the oars. Jack rowed vigorously, thinking that it was good practice for the time when he would go to the island.

'Well – here we are, safely back again,' said Bill, as the boat came to shore. The boys jumped out and pulled it in. The girls got out, bringing the thermos flask with them. Bill pulled the boat up the shore.

'Well, goodbye,' he said. 'We've had a fine time. Come along tomorrow, if you like, and I'll let you have a shot at taking the boat out by yourselves.'

'Oh, thanks!' cried the children, and Kiki echoed the words too. 'Oh, thanks!' she said, 'oh, thanks; oh, thanks; oh thanks!'

'Be quiet,' said Philip, with a laugh, but Kiki chanted the words all the way home. 'Oh, thanks; oh, thanks; oh, thanks; oh, thanks!'

'Did you have a nice afternoon?' asked Aunt Polly, when they went into the house.

'Lovely,' said Dinah. 'Is your headache better, Aunt Polly?'

'Not much,' said her aunt, who looked pale and

tired. 'I think I'll go to bed early tonight, if you'll take your uncle's supper in to him, instead of me, Dinah.'

'Yes, I will,' said Dinah, not liking the task very much, for she was rather afraid of her learned and peculiar uncle.

Joe came in at that moment and stared at the four children. 'Where you been?' he asked roughly. 'And where did you go this morning, after you went into the caves?'

'We came up to the house,' said Philip, putting on a surprised expression that infuriated Joe. 'Didn't you see us? And we've just come back from a picnic, Joe. Why all this concern for our whereabouts? Did you want to come with us?'

Joe made an angry noise, at once copied by Kiki, who then cackled out her maddening laughter. Joe gave the parrot a look of hatred and stalked out.

'Don't tease him,' said Aunt Polly wearily. 'He's really getting lazy. He never came near the house all the morning. Well – I'm going to bed.'

'Jack, you help me with Uncle Jocelyn's tray,'

said Dinah, when the supper was ready. 'It's heavy.
Philip's gone off somewhere as usual. He always
disappears when there's any job to be done.'

Jack took the heavy tray and followed Dinah as
she led the way to her uncle's study. She knocked
on the door. A voice grunted, and Dinah imagined
it said 'Come in.'

They went in, Kiki on Jack's shoulder as usual.

'Your supper, Uncle,' said Dinah. 'Aunt Polly's gone to bed. She's tired.'

'Poor Polly, poor dear Polly,' said Kiki, in a pitying tone. Uncle Jocelyn looked up, startled. He saw the parrot and picked up a paperweight.

Kiki at once flew out of the door, and Uncle Jocelyn put the paperweight down again. 'Keep that parrot out,' he said grumpily. 'Interfering bird. Put the tray down there. Who are you, young man?'

'I'm Jack Trent,' said Jack, surprised that anyone could be so forgetful. 'You saw me and my sister Lucy-Ann the day we came here, sir. Don't you remember?'

'Too many children in this house,' said Uncle Jocelyn, in a grumbling tone. 'Can't get any work done at all.'

'Oh, Uncle – you know we never disturb you,' said Dinah indignantly.

Uncle Jocelyn was bending over a big and very old map. Jack glanced at it.

'Oh,' he said, 'that's a map of part of this coast – and that's the Isle of Gloom, isn't it, sir?'

He pointed to the outline of the island, drawn carefully on the big map. Uncle Jocelyn nodded.

'Have you ever been there?' asked Jack eagerly. 'We saw it this afternoon, sir.'

'Never been there, and don't want to go either,' said Uncle Jocelyn surlily.

'I saw a Great Auk there this afternoon,' said Jack proudly.

This did not impress Uncle Jocelyn at all. 'Nonsense,' he said. 'Bird's been extinct for ages. You saw a razorbill. Don't be foolish, boy.'

Jack was annoyed. Only Lucy-Ann paid any attention to his great discovery, and she, he knew, would have believed him if he had said he had seen Santa Claus on the island. He stared sulkily at the untidy, frowning old man.

Uncle Jocelyn stared back. 'Could I see the map, please?' asked Jack suddenly, thinking that he might possibly see marked on it the entrance between the rocks.

'Why? Are you interested in that sort of thing?' asked Uncle Jocelyn, surprised.

'I'm very interested in the Isle of Gloom,' said Jack. 'Please – may I see the map, sir?'

'I've got a bigger one somewhere – showing only the island, in great detail,' said Uncle Jocelyn, quite pleased now to think that anyone should be interested in his maps. 'Let me see – where is it?'

Whilst he went to look for it, Jack and Dinah had a good look at the big map of the coast. There, lying off it, ringed by rocks, was the Isle of Gloom. It had a queer shape, rather like an egg with a bulge in the middle of one side, and its coast was very much indented. It lay almost due west of Craggy-Tops.

Jack pored over the map, feeling terribly excited. If only Uncle Jocelyn would lend it to him!

'Look,' he said to Dinah, in a low voice. 'Look. The ring of rocks is broken just there. See? I bet it's where I imagined the entrance was this afternoon. See that hill shown in the map? The entrance to the rocks is just about opposite. If ever we wanted to go there – and goodness knows I do – we need only look for that hill – it's the highest on the island, I should think – and then watch for the entrance to the rocks just opposite to the hill. Easy!'

'It looks easy on the map, but I bet it's a jolly sight more difficult when you get out on the sea,' said Dinah. 'You sound as if you mean to go there, Jack – but you know what we promised Bill Smugs. We can't break our promise.'

'I know that, idiot,' said Jack, who had never broken a promise in his life. 'I've got another plan. I'll tell you later.'

Much to the children's disappointment, Uncle Jocelyn could not find the large map of the island. He would not lend the other to Jack.

'Certainly not,' he said, looking quite shocked. 'It's a very, very old map – hundreds of years old. I wouldn't dream of handing it out to you. You'd damage it, or lose it or something. I know what children are.'

'You don't, Uncle,' said Dinah. 'You don't know what we are like a bit. Why, we hardly ever see you. Do lend us the map.'

But nothing would persuade the old man to part with his precious map. So, taking one last glance at the drawing of the island, with its curious ring of protecting rocks, and the one break in them, Jack and Dinah left the untidy, book-lined study.

'Don't forget your supper, Uncle,' called back Dinah as she shut the door. Uncle Jocelyn gave a grunt. He was already lost in his work again. The supper-tray stood unheeded beside him.

'I bet he'll forget all about it,' said Dinah. And she was right. When Aunt Polly went into the study the next day to tidy it as usual, there was the supper-tray standing on the table, complete with plate of meat and vegetables, and piece of pie and custard.

'You're worse than a child,' scolded Aunt Polly. 'Yes, you really are, Jocelyn.'

15

A Peculiar Happening – and a Fine Trip

That night Jack told the others his plan, and they were at first doubtful, and then thrilled and excited.

'Could we really find the entrance?' said Lucy-Ann, scared.

'Easily,' said Jack, who, once he had made up his mind about anything, would not recognise any difficulties at all. 'I saw the entrance this afternoon, I'm sure, and I certainly saw it on the map. So did Dinah.'

'So did Dinah, so did Dinah, so did Dinah,' chanted Kiki. Nobody took any notice of her. They all went on talking excitedly.

'You see, once I feel absolutely at home in handling Bill's boat, I shan't be a bit afraid of taking Joe's,' said Jack.

'He'll half kill you if he finds out,' said Philip. 'How

are you going to manage it without his knowing?'

'I shall wait till he takes the old car and goes shopping,' said Jack at once. 'I'd thought of that. As soon as he goes off in the car, I shall take out the boat, and hope to come back before he returns. If I don't – well, it just can't be helped. You'll have to distract his attention somehow – or lock him up in the cellar – or something.'

The others giggled. The idea of locking Joe up amused them.

'But look here,' said Philip, 'aren't we coming with you? You can't go alone.'

'I'm not taking the girls,' said Jack firmly. 'I don't mind any risk myself – but I won't risk everyone. I'd better take you, Philip.'

'I don't want you to take risks,' said poor Lucy-Ann, with tears in her eyes.

'Don't be such a baby,' said Jack. 'Why can't you be like Dinah, and not worry about me when I want to do something? Dinah doesn't bother about Philip taking risks, do you, Dinah?'

'No,' said Dinah, well aware that Philip could

take very good care of himself. 'All the same – I wish we could come.'

Lucy-Ann blinked back her tears. She didn't want to spoil things for Jack – but really, it was awful to think he might be wrecked or drowned. She wished with all her heart that Great Auks had never existed. If they hadn't existed they couldn't be extinct, and if they hadn't been extinct there wouldn't be all this excitement about finding one again.

Jack did not sleep much that night. He lay and thought about the island and its birds, and could hardly wait to sail off and see whether it really was a Great Auk or not he had spotted through his glasses that afternoon. He might get a lot of money if he caught the Great Auk. It couldn't fly, it could only swim. It might be so tame that it would let itself be caught. There might be three or four Great Auks. It would be simply wonderful to find out.

Jack got up and went to the window. He looked out to the west where the island lay. There was no moon that night, and he could see nothing at first.

But, as he gazed earnestly to the west, thinking hard of the island, he was astonished to see something distinctly unusual.

He blinked his eyes and looked again. It seemed as if a light was shining out there, over to the west where the island was. It went out slowly as he watched, and then came again. 'It *can't* be a real light,' said Jack. 'Anyway, it can't be a light on the island. It must be some ship a good way out, signalling.'

The light to the west faded again, and did not reappear. Jack pulled his head back, meaning to go to bed again, feeling sure that it must have been a ship's light he had seen.

But, before he could go back to his bed, something else attracted him. The narrow window on the opposite side, the one looking over the top of the cliff, was outlined in a soft light. Jack stared in amazement.

He ran to the window and looked out. The light came from the top of the rocky cliff. Someone had either built a fire there or had a bright lantern. Who could it be? And why show a light at night? Was it to signal to the ship out at sea?

Jack's room was the highest in Craggy-Tops, and the tower in which it was built jutted above the cliff-top. But though he craned his neck to look out as far as he could, he could not see what the light was on the top of the cliff, nor exactly where. He decided to find out.

He did not wake Philip. He put on shorts and coat and shoes and ran silently down the stairs. He was soon climbing the path to the top of the cliff. But when he got there, there was no light to be seen at all – no smell, even, of a fire. It was very puzzling.

The boy stumbled along the cliff – and suddenly he got the fright of his life. Someone clutched at him and held him fast.

'What you doing up here?' said Joe's voice, and he shook the boy till he had no breath left in his body. 'Go on – you tell me what you doing up here.'

Too frightened to think of anything but the truth, Jack blurted it out.

'I saw a light from the tower-room – and I came to see what it was.'

'I told you there was "things" on the cliff at night, didn't I?' said Joe, in a frightening voice. 'Well, those things show lights, and they wail and yell sometimes, and lord knows what else they do. Didn't I tell you not to wander out at night?'

'What are *you* out for?' asked Jack, beginning to recover from his fright.

Joe shook him again, glad to have got one of the children in his power. 'I come out to see what the light was too,' he growled. 'See? That's what I was out for, of course. But it's always those "things" making a disturbance and a trouble. Now, you promise me you'll never leave your bedroom no more at nights.'

'I shan't promise you anything,' said Jack, beginning to struggle. 'Let me go, you beast. You're hurting me.'

'I'll hurt you a mighty lot more, less you tell me you won't go out at nights,' threatened the man. 'I got a rope-end here, see? I been keeping it for you and Philip.'

Jack was afraid. Joe was immensely strong, spiteful and cruel. He struggled hard again, feeling Joe untying the rope he had around his waist.

It was Kiki that saved him. The parrot, missing Jack suddenly from the tower-room, where she had been sleeping peacefully on the perch that the boy had rigged up for her, had come in search of her master. She would not be separated from him for long, if she could help it.

Just as Jack was wondering whether it would be a good idea to bite Joe hard or not, Kiki swooped down with a glad screech. 'Kiki! Kiki! Bite him! Bite him!' yelled Jack.

The parrot gladly fastened her sharp curved beak into a very fleshy part of the man's arm. He let Jack go and gave an agonised yell. He hit out at Kiki, who was now well beyond reach, watching for a chance to attack again.

This time she tore at Joe's ear, and he yelled loudly. 'Call that bird off ! I'll wring her neck!'

Jack disappeared down the cliff path. When he was safely out of reach, he called Kiki.

'Kiki! Come on. You're a very good bird.'

Kiki took a last bite at Joe's other ear and then flew off with a screech. She flew to Jack's shoulder and made soft noises in his ear. He scratched her head gently as he made his way back to the house, his heart beating fast.

'Keep out of Joe's way, Kiki,' he said. 'He certainly *will* wring your neck now, if he can. I don't know what you did to him – but it must have been something very painful.'

Jack woke up Philip and told him what had happened. 'I expect the light was from a ship at sea,' he said, 'but I don't know what the other light was. Joe said he went up to see too, but he thought it was made by the "things" he is always talking about. Golly, I nearly got tanned by him, Philip. If it hadn't been for Kiki, I guess I'd have had a bad time.'

'Good old Kiki,' said Philip, and Kiki repeated his words in delight.

'Good old Kiki, good old Kiki, good old . . .'

'That's enough,' said Jack, and Kiki stopped. Jack snuggled deep into bed. 'I'm tired,' he said. 'I hope I soon go to sleep. I simply couldn't doze off before. I kept thinking and thinking of the Isle of Gloom.'

But it was not long before he was asleep, dreaming of a large map that had the island marked on it, then of a boat that was trying to get to the isle, and then of Joe clutching him and trying to pull back both him and the boat.

The children felt pleased the next morning when they remembered that Bill Smugs had said they could try out the boat by themselves. They set off early, having done all their jobs very quickly. Joe was in a bad temper that day. He slouched about, frowning, glaring at Jack and Kiki as if he would like to get hold of both of them.

For once in a way he did not follow them about or try to track them where they went. Aunt Polly was determined that he was going to do some work that morning, and she set him all kinds of tasks. He saw that it would be no good trying to evade them, so, very sulkily, he set to work, and the children were able to escape easily without being seen.

'I'm going to the town today,' said Bill, when

they arrived at his tumbledown shack. 'I simply must get hammer and nails and wood, and mend up my house a bit. Some more bits of wall have fallen down, and I spent last night with a gale rushing all round me – or what seemed like a gale in this small place. I must do a spot of mending. Do you want to come with me and do some shopping again too?'

'No, thank you,' said Jack at once. 'We would rather go out in the boat, please, Bill. It's quite a calm day. We will be very careful.'

'You'll remember your promise, of course,' said Bill, and looked at Jack sharply. The boy nodded.

'I won't go far out,' he said, and the others said the same. They saw Bill off in his car, and watched him going carefully down the bumpy way to join the rough-and-ready road that led to the town.

Then they went to get the boat. Bill had left it out on the rocks, in its hiding place. The children had not discovered why he liked to keep it there, but they imagined that he did not want it stolen when he was away from the place. They had to swim out to it, wrapping their dry clothes in an oilskin bag that Bill lent them for the purpose. Philip towed it behind him.

They reached the rocks and made their way over them to the flattish stretch where the boat was hauled up, well out of reach of the waves. They undid the oilskin bag and changed into dry things. They threw their bathing-suits into the boat and then pulled her down to the water.

The sea was deep around the rocks, and the boat slid neatly in, with hardly a splash. The children piled into her, and the two boys took the oars.

With a little trouble they rowed the big boat away from the rocks and out into open water. Then they faced the task of putting up the sail without Bill Smugs to help them.

'It ought to be easy enough to us,' panted Jack, tugging at various ropes. 'We did it yesterday by ourselves.'

But yesterday Bill had shouted directions at them. Now there was no one to help them if they got into a muddle. Still, they did get the sail up after a time. Dinah was nearly knocked overboard, but

just managed to save herself. She was very angry.

'You did that on purpose, Philip,' she said to her brother, who was still struggling with different ropes. 'Just you apologise! Bill said there wasn't to be any hanky-panky or silly tricks on board.'

'Shut up,' said Philip, getting suddenly caught in a rope that seemed determined to hang him. 'Jack, help me.'

'Take the tiller, Dinah,' said Jack. 'I'll help old Tufty.'

But it was Dinah who, suddenly seeing that Philip was indeed in difficulties, came to his rescue and untangled him.

'Thanks,' said Philip. 'Blow these ropes! I seem to have undone too many. Is the sail all right?'

It seemed to be. The wind filled it and the boat began to rush along. It was fun. The children felt important at being alone, managing the boat all by themselves. It was, after all, a very big boat for children to sail. Jack looked across the water to where the Isle of Gloom loomed up. One day he would go there – land on it – look around – and goodness knows what he might find! A picture of the Great Auk rose in his mind and in his excitement he gybed the boat round and the sail swung across, almost knocking off the heads of the crouching children.

'Idiot!' said Philip indignantly. 'Here, let me take the tiller. We shall all be in the water if you play about like that.'

'Sorry,' said Jack. 'I was just thinking of something – how I'd go off in Joe's boat. When do you think we could, Philip? In two or three days' time?'

'I should think we could sail Joe's boat all right by then,' said Philip. 'It's easy enough once you've got the knack and are quick enough. I'm getting to know the feel of the wind, and its strength – really feeling at home in the boat. Poor Lucy-Ann never will, though. Look how green she's gone.'

'I'm all right,' said Lucy-Ann valiantly. They had run into a choppy patch, and poor Lucy-Ann's tummy didn't like it. But nothing would ever persuade her to let the others go without her, even if she knew she was going to feel sick all the time. Lucy-Ann had plenty of pluck.

The children furled the sail after a time and got out the oars. They carefully remembered their promise and did not go very far away. They thought it would be a good thing to practise rowing for a while too.

So all of them took turns, and soon they could pull the boat along well, and make it go any way they liked, even without the rudder.

Then they put up the sail once more and sailed to shore, feeling very proud of themselves. When they came near the shore they saw Bill Smugs waving to them. He had already come back.

They sailed in to the beach, and pulled in the boat. 'Good!' said Bill. 'I was watching you out at sea. You did very well. Have another go tomorrow.'

'Oh, thanks,' said Jack. 'I suppose we couldn't have a try this afternoon too, could we? Dinah and Lucy-Ann wouldn't be able to, because they've got to do something for Aunt Polly. But Philip and I could come.'

The girls knew that Jack wanted to see if he and Philip were able to manage the boat by themselves, in preparation for going out alone in Joe's boat. So they said nothing, much as they would have liked to join in, and Bill Smugs said yes, the boys could go along that afternoon if they liked.

'I shan't come,' he said. 'I'm going to have a go at my radio set. It's gone wrong.'

Bill had a marvellous radio, the finest the boys had ever seen. It was set at the back of the old hut, and there was no station that Bill could not get. He would not allow the boys to tamper with it at all.

'Well, we'll be along this afternoon, then,' said Jack, pleased. 'It's awfully nice of you to lend us your boat like this, Bill. Really it is.'

'It's a pleasure,' said Bill Smugs, and grinned. Kiki imitated him.

'It's a pleasure, it's a pleasure, it's a pleasure, poor old Kiki, wipe your feet, never mind, never mind, it's a pleasure.'

'Oh – that reminds me,' said Jack, remembering his strange experience of the night before. 'Bill, listen to this.' He went off into a long account of his adventure on the cliff with Joe, and Bill Smugs listened with the greatest attention.

'So you saw lights?' he said. 'Out at sea – and on the cliff. Very interesting. I don't wonder you wanted to look into the matter. Joe apparently had the same curiosity about them. Well, if I may give you a bit of advice, it's this – don't get up against Joe more than you can help. I don't much like the sound of him. He sounds a dangerous sort of fellow.'

'Oh, he's just a bit grumpy and hates children and their games, but I don't think he'd really do us much harm,' said Philip. 'He's been with us for years.'

'Really?' said Bill, interested. 'Well, well – I expect your people would have a hard job to get anyone in Joe's place if he went. All the same – beware of him.'

The boys went off with the two girls. Philip was rather inclined to laugh at Bill's warning, but Jack took it to heart. He had not forgotten his fear the night before when the handyman had caught him.

'I think Bill's right, somehow,' thought Jack, with a little shiver. 'Joe could be a very dangerous sort of fellow.'

16

Strange Discoveries

The next three days the children worked hard at rowing and sailing, until they were perfectly at home in Bill's boat, and could handle it almost as well as Bill. He was pleased with them.

'I must say I do like to see children sticking to things, even if it means hard work,' he said. 'Even old Kiki has stuck to it too, sitting on the sail, over-balancing half the time, but not dreaming of letting you go by yourselves. And as for Lucy-Ann, she's the best of the lot, because she has had to fight seasickness a good part of the time.'

That afternoon, having first seen that Joe was safely in the yard at the back of the house, pumping up water from the deep well there, the children went to examine Joe's boat carefully, to see if they could possibly handle it themselves.

They stood and looked at it bobbing on the

water. It was bigger than Bill's, but not very much. They felt certain they would be all right in it.

'It's a pity Kiki can't row,' said Jack. 'She could take the third pair of oars and we could get along fine.'

'Fine,' said Kiki. 'Fine. God save the Queen.'

'Idiot,' said Philip affectionately. He was as fond of Kiki as Jack and Lucy-Ann were, and the bird went to him readily. 'I say, Freckles — I wonder when Joe is going to town again. I'm longing to try my hand at the boat; aren't you?'

'I should just think so,' said Jack. 'I keep on and on thinking of that Great Auk I saw. I shan't be happy till I've seen it close to.'

'Bet you won't find it,' said Philip. 'It would be awfully funny if you did, though — and came back with it cradled in your arms. Wouldn't Kiki be jealous?'

To the children's delight, Aunt Polly announced that Joe was going shopping the next day. 'So if you want anything, you must tell him,' she said. 'He has a long list of things to get for me — you can add anything you want to it, and give him the money.'

They put down a new torch battery on the list. Dinah had left her torch on one night and the battery was now no use. She must have a new one. Jack added another roll of film. He had been taking photographs of the sea-birds round Craggy-Tops, and now wanted a new film to take to the Isle of Gloom with him.

They waited anxiously for Joe to depart the next day. He seemed irritatingly slow. He started up the car at last and backed it out of the tumbledown shed where it lived. 'Now don't you children get into mischief while I'm gone,' he said, his sharp eyes watching them suspiciously. Perhaps he sensed that they were wishing him to be gone for reasons of their own.

'We never get into mischief,' said Philip. 'Have a good time – and don't hurry back.'

Joe scowled, put his foot on the accelerator and shot off at his usual breakneck speed. 'Can't think how the old car stands those bumps and jerks,' said Philip, watching it go across the cliff and disappear down to the road on the other side. 'Well – he's gone. Now, what about it? Our chance has come.'

In great excitement the children ran down to the beach, and made their way to the big boat. The boys got in. Dinah untied the rope and gave it a push.

'Take care of yourselves,' called Lucy-Ann anxiously, longing to jump into the boat with them. 'Do take care of yourselves.'

'Okay!' yelled back Jack, and Kiki echoed the word. 'Okay, okay, okay, shut the door and wipe your feet!'

The girls watched the boys rowing hard, and then they saw them put up the sail as soon as they were out on the open sea. There was a good wind and they were soon moving along at a fine speed.

'Off to the Isle of Gloom,' said Lucy-Ann. 'Well, I hope Jack brings back the Great Auk.'

'He won't,' said Dinah, whose common sense told her that it would indeed be a miracle if he did. 'Well, I hope they find the entrance to those awful rocks all right. They seem to be managing the boat well, don't they?'

'Yes,' said Lucy-Ann, straining her eyes to follow

the boat, which was now becoming difficult to see, owing to a haze over the water. The Isle of Gloom could not be seen at all. 'Oh dear – I do hope they'll get on well.'

The boys were having a fine time. They found that although Joe's boat was heavier and more awkward to manage than Bill's, it was not really difficult. There was quite enough wind and they were simply rushing through the water. It was most exhilarating to feel the up-and-down movement, and to hear the wind in the taut sail, and see the waves racing by.

'Nothing like a boat,' said Jack happily. 'One day I'll have one of my own.'

'They cost a lot of money,' said Philip.

'Well, I'll make a lot, then,' said Jack. 'Then I'll buy a fine boat of my own, and go sailing off to distant islands inhabited by nothing but birds, and won't I have a marvellous time!'

'I wish we could see the island,' said Philip. 'This haze is a nuisance. I hope we're going in the right direction.'

Before they saw the island, they heard the thundering of the waves on the ring of rocks around it. Then quite suddenly, after what seemed a very long time, the island loomed up, and the boys felt the spray from the breaking waves falling finely around them.

'Look out – we're heading straight for the rocks!' cried Philip in alarm. 'Take down the sail. We'll have to row. We can't manage the boat in this wind – it's got too strong. She's going too fast.'

They took down the sail, got out the oars and began to row. Jack tried to see the high hill. But it was much more difficult to spot the hill in reality than it had been to see it on the map. The hills seemed more or less the same size. The boys rowed round the ring of rocks, keeping well out of reach of the current that swept towards the island.

'There's a high hill – see, to the left,' suddenly said Jack. 'Pull towards there, Tufty. That's right. I believe that's the one we want.'

They pulled hard at their oars, panting and perspiring. Then, as the hill came right into view,

the boys saw, to their delight, a gap in the ring of rocks – a narrow gap, it is true, but decidedly an opening through which a boat might pass.

'Now – careful,' warned Philip. 'This is the tricky bit. Watch out. We may get swung off our course and run into the rocks. And anyway, although there are none showing just there, in the gap, there might be some just below the water that would rip the bottom from our boat. Careful, Freckles, careful!'

Jack was very careful. Everything depended on getting safely through the gap. The boys, their faces strained and anxious, rowed cautiously. Kiki didn't say a word. She knew that the boys were worried.

The gap or passage was narrow but long. It was anxious work getting the boat through. Various strong currents seemed to be doing their best to drive her to this side or that, and once the boys felt the bottom being scraped by some rock that was not far below the water.

'That was a narrow shave,' said Philip, in a low voice. 'Did you hear that nasty scrape?'

'I felt it too,' said Jack. 'Hallo – we seem to be all right now. I say, how marvellous, Tufty – we're in a channel of perfectly calm water!'

Beyond the rim of rocks was a channel or moat of brilliant blue, calm water, gleaming in the summer sun. It was strange to see it after the turbulence of the waves that raced over the rocks. They could hear the thunder of these still.

'Not far to the island now,' said Philip, thrilled. 'Come on – I'm frightfully tired – at least my arms are – but we simply *must* get to land. I'm longing to explore.'

They looked about for a good landing place. The island was very rocky indeed, but in one place there was a tiny cove where sand gleamed. The boys decided to land there.

It was quite easy to land and haul the boat a little way up the beach, though it took all the boys' strength to pull it up. But Bill had shown them the knack of hauling, and soon they were free to explore the deserted island.

They climbed the rocky cliff behind the little cove, and gazed over that side of the Isle of Gloom.

It was the number of birds that first took the boys' attention. There were thousands upon thousands, all kinds, all sizes, all shapes. The noise they made was tremendous. They took little notice of the boys, who stood watching them in wonder.

But they were not as tame as they had hoped. Sitting birds flew away as soon as the boys went near. They seemed as wild as those at Craggy-Tops. Jack was disappointed.

'Funny!' he said. 'I always thought that birds on a deserted island, where no men ever came, were completely tame. It says so in all my books, anyway. These are quite wild. They won't let us go really near them.'

There were a few trees to be seen, and what there were grew in sheltered spots, bent over sideways by the wind that blew across the island. Underfoot was a kind of wiry grass which grew in tufted patches here and there. But even that did not grow everywhere, and the bare rock thrust up in many places.

The boys left the cliff and walked inland, the cries of the thousands of birds in their ears. They made their way towards the hill that towered up in the centre of the isle.

'I want to see what those funny buildings are that I saw through the glasses,' said Jack, remembering. 'And oh dear, I do want to find a Great Auk. I haven't seen a sign of one yet. I keep on looking and looking.'

Poor Jack was in a terrible state of excitement, expecting to see a Great Auk at any moment, and, instead, seeing all kinds of birds he had already seen at Craggy-Tops. It *was* disappointing. He hadn't expected to see a procession of Great Auks – but one, just one, would have been marvellous.

There were plenty of big razorbills with their curiously-shaped beaks, plenty of skuas, gulls, cormorants and other birds. It was a paradise of sea-birds, and Jack was lost in wonder at the number of them. How he would like to spend a few days on this island, watching and taking photographs!

They came to the hills, and found a pass between them. Here there was more grass and a few tiny wild flowers, sea-pinks and others. One or two stunted birches grew on the hillsides.

Between the hills lay a small valley, and in it was a stream, running off into the sea on the other side of the island. The boys went to have a look at it because it seemed rather a curious colour.

It certainly was a strange colour. 'Sort of bright bluey-green,' said Jack, puzzled. 'I wonder why. I say, look! – there are those queer buildings, up on that hill. And do you notice, Tufty, how the rocks change in colour here? They are not black any more, but green. And some of them look like sandstone. It's queer, isn't it?'

'I don't think I like this island much,' said Philip, with a shudder. 'It feels lonely and odd – and sort of bad.'

'You've been listening to old Joe's tales too much,' said Jack, with a laugh, though he himself did not like the 'feel' of the island either. It was so mournful and desolate, and the only sounds to be heard so far inland were the incessant cries of the sea-birds circling overhead.

They climbed halfway up a hill to see the 'buildings'. It was difficult to make out what they were, they were so old and broken down – not much more than heaps of stones or rocks. They did not look as if they ever could have been places to live in.

And then, close to one of these 'buildings', Philip discovered something strange. He called Jack in excitement.

'I say! Come and look here! There's a terrific hole going right down into the earth – simply terrifically deep!'

Jack ran over to the hole and peered down it. It was a large hole, about six feet round, and it went so far down into the earth that the boys could not possibly see the bottom of it.

'What's it for?' said Philip. 'Is it a well, do you think?'

The boys dropped a stone down to see if they could hear a splash. But none came. Either it was not a well, or it was so deep that the sound of the splash could not be heard.

'I shouldn't like to fall down there,' said Philip. 'Look! – there's a ladder going down – awfully old and broken – but still, a ladder.'

'It's a mystery,' said Jack, puzzled. 'Let's go and look around a bit. We might find something to help us to clear up such a peculiar problem. A shaft going down into the depths of the earth, in a lonely island like this! Whatever was it made for?'

17

Joe Is Angry

To the boys' intense surprise, they found more of the deep narrow holes, all of them near the curious old 'buildings'. 'They can't be wells,' said Jack. 'That's impossible. No one would want so many. They must be shafts, sunk down deep into the earth here, for some good reason.'

'Do you think there were mines?' asked Philip, remembering that coal mines always had shafts bored down through the earth, so that men might go down and get the coal. 'Do you think there are old mines here? Coal mines, for instance?'

'No, not coal,' said Jack. 'I can't imagine what. We'll have to find out. I expect your uncle knows. Wouldn't it be exciting if it was a *gold* mine! You never know.'

'Well, it must have been worked out hundreds of years ago,' said Philip. 'There wouldn't be any gold left now, or it would still be worked. I say – shall we go down and see what there is to be seen?'

'I don't know,' said Jack doubtfully. 'The old ladders aren't much good, are they? We might fall hundreds of feet down – and that would be the end of us.'

'What a pity, what a pity!' remarked Kiki.

'Yes, it *would* be a pity,' said Philip, with a grin. 'Well, perhaps we'd better not. Hallo! – here's another shaft, Jack – a bit bigger one.'

The boys peered down this big one. It had a much better ladder than the others. They went down it a little way, feeling very daring. They soon came up again, for they did not like the darkness and the shut-in feeling.

And then they made a discovery that surprised them even more than the shafts. Not far off, piled under an overhanging bit of rock, were some empty meat and fruit tins.

This was such an extraordinary find that the boys could hardly believe their eyes. They stood and stared at the tins, and Kiki flew down to inspect them to see if there was anything left to eat.

'Where *do* you suppose those came from?' asked Jack at last. 'What a queer thing! Some are very rusty – but others seem quite new. Who could come to this island – and why – and where do they live?'

'It's a mystery,' said Philip. 'Let's have a jolly good look all round whilst we're here, and see if we can find anyone. Better go carefully, because it's quite plain that whoever lives here doesn't want it known.'

So the boys made a careful tour of the island, but saw nothing and nobody that could explain the mystery of the pile of tins. They wondered at the green rocks on the southward side of the island, and again puzzled over the green colour of the stream that ran into the sea there. There were many more birds on the seaward side, and Jack kept a sharp look-out for the Great Auk. But he did not see one, which was very disappointing.

'Aren't you going to take any photos?' asked Philip. 'You said you were. Hurry up, because we oughtn't to be much longer.'

'Yes – I'll take a few,' said Jack, and hid behind a convenient rock to snap a few young birds. Then, having one more film left, a thought struck him.

'I'll take a snap of that pile of tins,' he said. 'The girls mightn't believe us if we bring home such a queer tale, but they'll believe it all right if we show them the photo.'

So he snapped the pile of tins too, and then, with one last look down the big, silent shaft, the boys made their way back to the boat. There it lay, just out of reach of the water.

'Well, let's hope we make as good a trip home as we did coming out,' said Jack. 'I wonder if Joe is back yet. I hope to goodness that the girls have dealt with him somehow if he is.'

They pulled the boat into the water and got in. They rowed over the smooth moat to the exit between the rocks, where spray was being sent high into the air from waves breaking on either side. They managed to avoid the rock that had scraped the bottom of the boat before, and rowed quite easily out of the passage.

They had some trouble just outside, where the sea was very choppy indeed. The wind had changed a little, and the sea was rougher. They put up the sail and ran home in great style, exulting in the feel of the wind on their cheeks and the spray on their faces.

As they got near the shore after their long run, they saw the two girls waiting for them, and they waved. Dinah and Lucy-Ann waved back. Soon the boat slid to its mooring-place and the boys got out and tied it up.

'Did you find the Great Auk?' cried Lucy-Ann.

'Is Joe back?' asked Philip.

'You've been ages,' said Dinah, impatient to hear everything.

'We've had a fine adventure,' said Philip. 'Is Joe back?'

All these questions were asked at the same moment. The most important one was – was Joe back?

'Yes,' said Dinah, with a giggle. 'He came back about an hour ago. We were watching for him.

Luckily, he went straight down into the cellar with some boxes he brought back in the car, and we followed him. He opened that inner door and went into the back cellar with the boxes – and the cellar where the trap-door is – and we remembered where you'd put the key of that door, got in, and locked him in. He's banging away there like anything.'

'Good for you!' said the boys, pleased. 'Now he won't know we've been out in his boat. But how on earth are we going to let him out without his knowing we've locked him in?'

'You'll have to think of something,' said Dinah. The boys walked up to the house, thinking hard.

'We'd better slip down quietly and unlock the door when he's having a rest,' said Philip at last. 'He can't keep banging at the door for ever. As soon as he stops for a bit of rest, I'll quietly put the key in the lock and unlock the door. Then I'll slip upstairs again. The next time he tries the door, it will open – but he won't know why.'

'Good!' said the others, pleased. It seemed a very simple way of setting Joe free without his

guessing that it had anything to do with them.

Philip took the key and went down into the cellar as quietly as he could. As soon as he got down there he heard Joe hammering on the door. The boy waited till he had stopped for breath, and then pushed the big key quietly into the lock. He heard Joe coughing, and turned the key at the same moment, and then withdrew it. The door was unlocked now – and Joe could come out when he wanted to. Philip shot across the cellar to the steps, ran up them, out into the kitchen, and joined the others.

'He'll be out in a minute,' he panted. 'Let's slip up on to the cliff, and as soon as we see Joe again, we'll walk down to the house, pretending we are just back from a walk. That will puzzle him properly.'

So they all ran up to the cliff, lay down on the top, and peeped over to see when Joe appeared. In low voices the boys told the girls all they had found on the Isle of Gloom.

The two girls listened in amazement. Deep holes in the earth – a stream that was bright green – a pile of food tins – how very strange! No one had expected anything like that. It was birds they had gone to see.

'We simply must go back again and find out what those shafts lead down to,' said Jack. 'We'll find out too if there were once mines of some sort there. Perhaps your Uncle Jocelyn would know, Dinah.'

'Yes, he would,' said Dinah. 'Golly, I wish we could get hold of that old map of the island he spoke about – the one he couldn't find. It might show us all kinds of interesting things, mightn't it?'

Kiki suddenly gave one of her express-train screeches, which meant she had sighted her enemy, Joe. The children saw him down below, looking all round, evidently for them. They scrambled to their feet and walked jauntily down the path to the house.

Joe saw them and came to meet them, fury in his face. 'You locked me in,' he said. 'I'll tell Miss Polly of you. You ought to be whipped.'

'Locked you in!' said Philip, putting a look of sheer amazement on his face. 'Where did we lock you in? Into your room?'

'Down in the cellar,' said Joe, in a furious voice. 'Here's Miss Polly. I'll tell of you. Miss Polly, these children locked me into the cellar.'

'Don't talk nonsense,' said Aunt Polly. 'You know there is no lock on the cellar door. The children have been for a walk – look at them just coming back to the house – how can you say they locked you in? You must be imagining things.'

'They locked me in,' said Joe sulkily, suddenly

remembering that the inner cellar was his own secret place and that he had better not go into any details, or Aunt Polly would go down and discover the door he had so carefully hidden.

'I didn't lock him in, Aunt Polly,' said Philip earnestly. 'I've been ever so far away all morning.'

'So have I,' said Jack, quite truthfully. Aunt Polly believed them, and as she knew that the four children were always together, she imagined that the girls had been with them. So how could any of them have played a trick on Joe? And anyway, thought Aunt Polly, there *was* no lock on the door to the cellar, so what in the wide world did Joe mean? He really must be getting confused.

'Go and do your work, Joe,' she said sharply. 'You always seem to have your knife into the children, accusing them of this and that. Leave them alone. They're good children.'

Joe thought otherwise. He gave one of his famous scowls, made an angry noise, beautifully copied by Kiki, and returned to the kitchen.

'Don't take any notice of him,' said Aunt Polly.

'He's very bad-tempered, but he's quite harmless.'

The children went back into the house, winking at one another. It was nice to have Aunt Polly on their side. All the same, Joe was piling up grievances against them. They must look out.

'Funny,' thought Jack. 'Aunt Polly says Joe is quite harmless – and Bill Smugs says he's a dangerous fellow. One of them is certainly wrong.'

18

Off to the Island Again

What should be done next? Should they tell Bill Smugs of their adventure? Would he be angry because they had evaded their promise, without actually breaking it, and gone out to the island in someone else's boat? The children decided that he might be very angry. He had great ideas of honour and promises and keeping one's word.

'Well, so have we,' said Jack. 'I wouldn't have broken my promise. I didn't. I just found a way round it.'

'Well, you know what grown-ups are,' said Dinah. 'They don't think the same way as we do. I expect when we grow up, we shall think like them – but let's hope we remember what it was like to think in the way children do, and understand the boys and girls that are growing up when *we're* men and women.'

'You're talking like a grown-up already,' said Philip in disgust. 'Stop it.'

'Don't talk to me like that,' flared Dinah. 'Just because I was talking a bit of sense.'

'Shut up,' said Philip, and got a box on the ear from Dinah immediately. He gave her a slap that sounded like a pistol-shot and she yelled.

'Beast!' she said. 'You know boys shouldn't hit girls.'

'I shouldn't hit ordinary decent girls, like Lucy-Ann,' said Philip. 'But you're just too bad-tempered for words. You ought to know by now that if you box my ears you'll get a jolly good slap. Serves you right.'

'Jack, tell him he's a beast,' said Dinah; but Jack couldn't help giving Dinah some advice.

'You should keep your hands to yourself,' he said to her. 'You're so quick at dishing out ear-boxes, and you ought to know by now that Philip won't stand for it.'

Lucy-Ann looked distressed. She hated these quarrels between the brother and sister. Philip put his hand into his pocket and pulled out a box in which he had kept an extraordinarily tame beetle for days. Dinah knew he meant to open the box and put the beetle close to her. She gave a scream and rushed out of the room.

Philip put the box back into his pocket, after letting the enormous beetle have a run on the table. Wherever he held out his finger the beetle ran to it in delight. It really was amazing the way all creatures liked Philip.

'You oughtn't to keep it in a box,' said Lucy-Ann. 'I'm sure it hates it.'

'Well, watch, then,' said Philip, and put the box out on the table again. He opened it, took out the beetle, and put it at the other end of the big table. He put the box, with its lid a little way open, on to the middle of the table. The beetle, having explored the top of the table thoroughly, made its way to the box, examined it, and then climbed into it and settled down peacefully.

'There you are!' said Philip, shutting the box and putting it back into his pocket. 'It wouldn't go deliberately back into its box if it hated it, would it?'

'Well – it must be because it likes being with you,' said Lucy-Ann. 'Most beetles would hate it.'

'Philip is a friend to everything,' said Jack, with a grin. 'I believe he could train fleas and keep a circus of them.'

'I shouldn't like that,' said Lucy-Ann, looking disgusted. 'Oh dear, I wonder where Dinah has gone off to. I wish you wouldn't quarrel like this. We were having such a nice talk about what to do next.'

Dinah had left the room in a rage, her arm stinging from Philip's slap. She wandered down the passage that led to her uncle's room, thinking up horrid things to do to her brother. Suddenly her uncle's door opened and he peered out.

'Oh, Dinah – is that you? The ink pot here is empty,' he said, in a peevish voice. 'Why doesn't somebody fill it?'

'I'll get the ink bottle for you,' said Dinah, and went to get it from her aunt's cupboard. She took it to the study and filled her uncle's ink pot. As she turned to go, she noticed a map on a chair nearby. It was the one that her uncle could not find before – the large one of the Isle of Gloom. The little girl looked at it with interest.

'Oh, Uncle – here's that map you told us about. Uncle, do tell me – used there to be mines on the island?'

'Now, where did you hear that?' said her uncle, astonished. 'That's old history. Yes, there used to be mines, hundreds of years ago. Copper mines – rich ones too. But they were all worked out years ago. There's no copper there now.'

Dinah pored over the map. To her delight it showed where the shafts were, that ran deep down into the earth. How the boys would like to see that map!

Her uncle turned to his work, forgetting all about Dinah. She picked up the map and slipped out of the room very quietly. How pleased Philip would be with the map!

She had forgotten all her anger. That was the best part about Dinah – she bore no malice, and her furies were soon over. She ran down the passage to the room where she had left the others. She flung open the door and burst in.

The others were amazed to see her smiling and excited face. Lucy-Ann could never get used to the quick changes in Dinah's moods. Philip looked at her doubtfully, not smiling.

Dinah remembered the quarrel. 'Oh,' she said, 'I'm sorry I boxed your ears, Philip. Look here – I've got that old map of the island. What do you think of that? And Uncle Jocelyn told me there *were* mines there, once – copper ones – very rich. But they are worked out now. So those shafts must have led down to the mines.'

'Golly!' said Philip, taking the map from Dinah's hands and spreading it out. 'What a map!

Oh, Dinah, you *are* clever!'

He gave his sister a squeeze and Dinah glowed. She quarrelled with her brother continually, but she loved getting a word of praise from him. The four children bent over the map.

'There's the gap in the rocks – as plain as anything,' said Dinah. The boys nodded.

'It must have always been there,' said Jack. 'I suppose that's the only way the old miners could use to go to and from the island. How thrilling to think of their boats going and coming – taking food there, bringing back copper! Golly, I'd like to go down and see what they are like.'

'Look, all the old shafts are marked,' said Philip, and he placed his finger on them. 'There's the one we must have found those tins near, Freckles, look! – and here's the stream. And now I know why it's green. It's coloured by the copper deposits still in the hills, I bet.'

'Well, perhaps there is still copper there, then,' said Dinah, in great excitement. 'Copper nuggets! Oooh, I wish we could find some.'

'Copper is found in veins,' said Philip, 'but I think it's found whole, in nuggets too. They might be valuable. I say – shall we, just for a lark, go across to the island, go down to the mines, and hunt about a bit? Who knows, we *might* find nuggets of copper.'

'There won't be any,' said Jack. 'No one would leave a mine if there were still copper to be worked. It's been deserted for hundreds of years.'

'There's something stuck on to the back of the map,' said Lucy-Ann suddenly. The children turned it over, and saw a smaller map fastened to the larger one. They smoothed it out to look at it – and then Philip gave an exclamation.

'Of course! It's an underground map of the island – a map of the mines. Look at these passages and galleries and these draining-channels to take away water. Golly, part of these mines are below the level of the sea.'

It was weird to look at a map that showed the maze of tunnels under the surface of the island. There had evidently been a vast area mined, some of it under the sea itself.

'This section is right under the bed of the sea,' said Jack, pointing. 'How queer to work there, and know that all the time the sea is heaving above the rocky ceiling over your head!'

'I shouldn't like it,' said Lucy-Ann, shivering. 'I'd be afraid it would break through and flood where I was working.'

'Look here, we simply must go over to the island again,' said Philip excitedly. 'Do you know what I think? I think that people are working in those mines now.'

'Whatever makes you think that?' said Dinah.

'Well, those food tins,' said Philip. 'Someone eats food there, out of tins. And we couldn't see them anywhere, could we? So it must be that they were down in the mines, working. I bet you that's the solution of the mystery.'

'Let's go over to Bill and tell him all about it tomorrow, and take this map to show him,' said Dinah, thrilled. 'He will tell us what to do. I don't feel like exploring the mines by ourselves. I somehow feel I'd like Bill with us.'

'No,' said Jack suddenly. 'We won't tell Bill.'

The others looked at him in surprise.

'Why ever not?' demanded Dinah.

'Well – because I've suddenly got an idea,' said Jack. 'I believe it's a friend of Bill's – or friends – working in those mines. I believe Bill's come here to be near them – to take food over – and that sort of thing. I bet he uses his boat for that. It must be a secret, I should think. Well – he wouldn't be too pleased if we knew his secret. He'd never let us go out in his boat again.'

'But, Jack – you're exaggerating. Bill's only come for a holiday. He's bird-watching,' said Philip.

'He doesn't *really* do much bird-watching,' said Jack. 'And though he listens to me when I rave about the birds here, he doesn't talk much about them himself – not like I would if someone gave me the chance. And we don't know what his business is. He's never told us. I bet you anything you like that he and his friends are trying to work a copper mine over on the island. I don't know who the mines belong to – if they *do* belong to anyone – but

I guess if it was suspected that there was still copper there, the people who made the discovery would keep it secret on the chance of mining some good copper nuggets themselves.'

Jack paused, quite out of breath. Kiki murmured the new word she had heard.

'Copper, copper, copper. Spare a copper, copper, copper.'

'Isn't she clever?' said Lucy-Ann; but no one paid any attention to Kiki. The matters being discussed were far too important to be interrupted by a parrot.

'Let's ask Bill Smugs straight out,' suggested Dinah, who always liked to get things clear. She disliked mysteries that couldn't be solved.

'Don't be an ass,' said Philip. 'Jack's already told you why it would be best not to let Bill know we know his secret. Maybe he'll tell us himself one day – and won't he be surprised to know that we guessed it!'

'We'll go over in Joe's boat again soon,' said Jack. 'We'll go down that big shaft and explore a bit. We'll soon find out if anyone is there. We'll take this map with us so that we don't lose our way. It shows the underground passages and galleries very clearly.'

It was exciting to talk over these secrets. When could they go off to the island again? Should they take the girls this time – or not?

'Well, I think we shall manage even better this time,' said Philip. 'There wasn't much danger really last time, once we found the passage through the ring of rocks. I'm pretty certain we shall get to the island easily next time. We can take the girls as well.'

Dinah and Lucy-Ann were thrilled. They longed for a chance to go at once, but Joe did not leave Craggy-Tops long enough for them to take his boat. However, he went out in it himself two or three times.

'Are you going fishing?' asked Philip. 'Why don't you take us with you?'

'Not going to bother myself with children like you,' said the man, in his surly way, and set off in his boat. He sailed out such a long way that his boat disappeared into the haze that always seemed to hang about the western horizon.

'He may have gone to the island, for all we can see,' said Jack. 'He just disappears. I hope he brings some fish back for supper tonight.'

He did. His boat returned after tea and the children helped to take in a fine catch of fish. 'You might have taken us too, you mean thing,' said Dinah. 'We could have let lines down as well.'

The next day Joe departed to the town again, much to the children's joy. 'He's got the day off,' said Aunt Polly. 'You will have to do some of his jobs. You boys can pump up the water for the day.'

The boys went off to the well and let down the heavy bucket, unwinding the chain till the bucket reached the water. Jack peered over the edge.

'Just like one of those shafts over in the island,' he said. 'Wind up, wind up, Tufty – here goes!'

The children hurried over all the work that Aunt Polly set them to do. Then, making certain that the car was gone out of the garage, they begged a picnic lunch from Aunt Polly and raced down to Joe's boat.

They undid the rope and pushed off, the two boys rowing hard. As soon as they were out on the open sea, up went the sail. 'Off we go to the Isle of Gloom,' said Dinah, in delight. 'Gosh, I'm glad we're coming with you this time, Jack. It was hateful being left behind last time.'

'Did you bring the torches?' asked Philip of Lucy-Ann. She nodded. 'Yes. They're over there with the lunch.'

'We shall need them down the mines,' said Philip, with an air of excitement. What an adventure this was – to be going down old, old mines, where possibly men might be secretly hunting for copper. Philip shivered deliciously.

The sailing-boat, handled most expertly by the four children, went along well and they made very good time indeed. It did not seem to be very long before the island loomed up out of the usual haze.

'Hear the waves banging on the rocks?' said Jack. The girls nodded. This was the dangerous part.

They hoped the boys would find the rock passage as easily as before, and go in safely.

'There's the big hill,' said Jack suddenly. 'Down with the sail. That's right – easy does it. Look out for that rope, Lucy-Ann. No, not that one – that's right.'

The sail was down. The boys took the oars and began to row cautiously towards the gap in the rocks. They knew where it was now. Into it they went, looking out for the rock that lay near the surface, ready to avoid it. It did scrape the bottom slightly and Lucy-Ann looked frightened. But soon they were in the calm moat of water that ran gleaming all round the island, between the shore and the ring of rocks.

Lucy-Ann heaved a sigh of relief. What with feeling a bit seasick and scared, she had gone quite pale. But now she recovered quickly as she saw the island itself so near.

They landed safely and pulled the boat up on to the shore. 'Now we make for the hills,' said Jack. 'My word, look at the thousands of birds again!

I never in my life saw such a lot. If only I could see that Great Auk!'

'Perhaps I'll see one for you,' said Lucy-Ann, wishing with all her heart that she could. 'Philip, where's that green-coloured stream – and the pile of tins? Anywhere near here?'

'You'll see soon,' said Philip, striding ahead. 'We go through this little pass in the hills.'

Soon they could see the bright green stream running in the valley among the hills. Jack paused and took his bearings. 'Wait a bit. Where exactly was that big shaft?'

The girls had already exclaimed over the other holes in the ground, and the queer tumbledown erections beside them. 'There must have been some sort of shaft-head,' said Jack, considering. 'Now, where's that pile of tins? It was somewhere near here. Oh – there's the shaft, girls!'

Everyone hurried to the big round hole and peered down it. There was no doubt but that the ladder leading down it was in very good condition. 'This is the shaft the men are using,' said Philip.

'It's the only one whose ladder is safe.'

'Don't talk too loudly,' said Jack, in a low voice. 'You don't know how sound might carry down this shaft.'

'Where are those tins you told us about?' said Lucy-Ann.

'Over there – by that rock,' said Philip, pointing. 'Go and see them if you want to.'

He shone his torch down the shaft, but could see very little. It looked rather sinister and forbidding. What was it like down there? Were there really men down there? The children mustn't be discovered by them – grown-ups were always angry when children poked their noses into matters that didn't concern them.

'Jack – I can't find the tins,' said Lucy-Ann. Philip made an impatient noise. He strode over to show them the pile.

Then he stopped in astonishment. The place under the rock was empty. There was nothing there at all. The tins had been removed.

'Look at that, Jack,' said Philip, forgetting to

speak softly. 'All those tins have gone. Who took them? Well – that just *shows* there are people on this island – people who have been here since we last came too. I say – isn't this exciting!'

19

Down in the Copper Mines

Lucy-Ann looked round her fearfully as if she half expected to see somebody hiding behind a rock.

'I don't like to think there may be people here we don't know anything about,' she said.

'Don't be silly,' said Jack. 'They're down in the mines. Shall we go down this shaft now, and see what we can discover?'

The girls didn't like the look of it, but Lucy-Ann felt that it would be worse to stay up above ground than it would be to go down and keep with the boys. So she said she would go, and Dinah, who wasn't going to be left all alone, promptly said she would go too.

Philip spread the map of the underground mines out on the ground, and they all knelt down and studied it. 'See – this shaft goes down to the centre of a perfect maze of passages and galleries,' said Philip. 'Shall we take this passage here? – it's a sort of main road, and leads to the mines that were worked right under the sea.'

'Oh no, don't let's go there,' said Lucy-Ann, in alarm. But the other three voted to go there, so the matter was decided.

'Now, Kiki, if you come with us, you are not to make a noise,' warned Jack. 'Else if we go anywhere near the miners, they will hear you, and we shall be discovered. See?'

'Eena meena mina mo,' said Kiki solemnly, and scratched her poll hard.

'You're a silly bird,' said Jack. 'Now mind what I've told you – don't you dare to screech or shout.'

They went to the head of the shaft. They all peered down, feeling rather solemn. An adventure was exciting, but somehow this one seemed a bit frightening, all of a sudden.

'Come on,' said Philip, beginning to go down the ladder. 'Nothing can happen to us really, even if we are discovered. After all, we first came to this island to see if we could find a Great Auk for Freckles.

Even if we were caught we could say that we'd keep our mouths shut. If the men are friends of Bill Smugs, they must be decent fellows. We can always say we are his friends.'

They all began to climb down the long, long shaft. Before they were halfway down they wished they had never begun their descent. They had not guessed they would have to go so far. It was like climbing down to the middle of the earth, down, down, down in the darkness, which was lit now by the beams from four torch lights.

'Everyone all right?' asked Philip, rather anxiously. 'I should think we must be near the bottom now.'

'My arms are terribly tired,' said poor Lucy-Ann, who was not so strong as the others. Dinah was as big and strong as any boy, but Lucy-Ann was not.

'Stop a little and rest,' said Jack. 'Golly, Kiki feels heavy on my shoulder. That's because my arms are a bit tired too, I expect, with holding on to the ladder-rungs.'

They rested a little and then went on downwards. Then Philip gave a low exclamation.

'I say! I'm at the bottom!'

With great thankfulness the others joined him. Lucy-Ann promptly sat down on the ground, for her knees were aching now, as well as her arms. Philip flashed his torch around.

They were in a fairly wide passage. The walls and ceiling were of rock, gleaming a coppery colour in the light of the torches. From the main passage branched many galleries or smaller passages.

'We'll do as we said and keep to this main passage, which looks like a sort of main road of the mines,' said Philip.

Jack flashed his torch down a smaller passage. 'Look!' he said. 'The roof has fallen in there. We couldn't go down that way if we wanted to.'

'Golly, I hope the roof of *this* passage won't fall in on top of us,' said Lucy-Ann, looking up at it in alarm. In places it was propped up by big timbers, but mostly it was of hard rock.

'Come on – we're safe enough,' said Jack impatiently. 'I say – isn't it thrilling to be hundreds of feet below the earth, down in a copper mine as old as the hills!'

'It's funny that the air is quite good here, isn't it?' said Dinah, remembering the musty-smelling air in the secret passage at Craggy-Tops.

'There must be good airways in these mines,' said Philip, trying to remember how the airways in coal mines worked. 'That's one of the first things that men think about when they begin to work mines underground – how to get draughts of air moving down the tunnels they make – and channels to drain off any water that might collect and flood the mine.'

'I'd hate to work in a mine,' said Lucy-Ann, shivering. 'Philip, are we under the sea yet?'

'Not yet,' said Philip. 'About halfway there, I should think. Hallo, here's a well-worked piece – quite a big cave!'

The passage suddenly opened out into a vast open cave that showed many signs of being worked by men. Marks of tools stood out here and there in the rock, and Jack, with a delighted exclamation, darted to a corner and picked up what looked like a small hammer-top made of bronze.

'Look,' he said proudly to the others. This must be part of a broken tool used by the ancient miners – it's made of bronze – a mixture of copper and tin. My word, won't the boys at school envy me this!'

That made the others look around eagerly as well, and Lucy-Ann made a discovery that interested everybody very much. It was not an ancient bronze tool – it was a stub of pencil, bright yellow in colour.

'Do you know who this belongs to?' said Lucy-Ann, her green eyes gleaming in the torchlight like a cat's. 'It belongs to Bill Smugs. I saw him writing notes with it the other day. I know it's Bill's.'

'Then he must have been down here and dropped it by accident,' said Philip, thrilled. 'Golly, our guess was right, then! He's no bird-watcher – he's living on the coast with his car and his boat because he's friends with the men working this old mine, and brings them food and stuff. Artful old Bill – he never told us a word about it.'

'Well, you don't go blabbing everything out to children you meet,' said Dinah. 'Well, well – how surprised he would be if he knew we knew his secret! I wonder if he's down here now?'

'Course not, silly,' said Philip, at once. 'His boat wasn't on the shore, was it? And there's no other way of getting here except by boat.'

'I forgot that,' said Dinah. 'Anyway – I don't feel afraid of meeting the secret miners now that we know they are friends of Bill's. All the same, we won't let them know we're here if we can help it.

They might think that children couldn't be trusted, and be rather cross about it.'

They examined the big cave closely. The ceiling was propped up with big old timbers, some of them broken now, so that the roof was gradually falling in. A number of hewn out steps led to a cave above, but the roof of that had fallen in and the children could not get into it.

'Do you know what I think?' said Jack suddenly, stopping to face the others behind him, as they examined the cave. 'I believe that light I saw out to sea the other night *wasn't* from a ship at all – it was from this island. The miners were giving a signal to say that they had finished their food and wanted more – and the light from the cliff was flashed by Bill to say he was bringing more.'

'Yes – but the light came from *our* cliff, not from Bill's cliff,' objected Philip.

'I know – but you know jolly well that it's only from the highest part of the cliff that anyone signalling from the cove side of the island could be seen,' said Jack. 'If somebody stood on that hill in the middle of the island and made a bonfire or waved a powerful lamp, it could only be seen from our cliff, and not from Bill's. So Bill must have gone to our cliff that night and answered the signal.'

'I believe you're right,' said Philip. 'Old Bill must have been wandering about that night, behind Craggy-Tops – and you saw his signalling light and so did Joe. No wonder old Joe says there are "things" wandering about at night and is scared of them! He must often have heard Bill and seen lights, and not known what they were.'

'I expect Bill went off to the island in his boat, as soon as he could, with fresh food,' said Jack. 'And he took away the pile of old tins. That explains why it is they are gone. Artful old Bill! What a fine secret he has – and we are the only people who know it!'

'I do wish we could tell him we know it,' said Lucy-Ann. 'I don't see why we can't. I'm sure he'd rather know that we knew it.'

'Well – we could sort of say a few things that will make him guess we know it, perhaps,' said Philip. 'Then if he guesses, he'll own up, and we'll have a good talk about the mines, and Bill will tell us all kinds of exciting things.'

'Yes, that's what we'll do,' said Jack. 'Come on – let's explore a bit further. I feel as if I know this cave by heart.'

The passage swerved suddenly to the left after a bit, and Philip's heart gave a thump. He knew, by the map, that when the main passage swerved left, they were going under the sea-bed itself. It was somehow very thrilling to be walking under the deep sea.

'What's that funny noise?' asked Dinah. They all listened. There was a curious, far-off booming noise that never stopped.

'Miners with machines?' said Philip. Then he suddenly knew what it was. 'No – it's the sea booming away above our heads! That's what it is!'

So it was. The children stood and listened to the muffled, faraway noise. Boom-boooom, boom. That was the sea, moving restlessly over the rocky bed, maybe pounding over rocks in its way, talking with its continual, rhythmical voice.

'It's funny to be under the sea itself,' said Lucy-Ann, half frightened. She shivered. It was so dark, and the noise was so strange. 'Isn't it awfully warm down here?' she said, and the others agreed with her. It certainly was hot down in the old copper mines.

They went on their way down the passage, keeping to the main one, and avoiding all the many galleries that spread out continually sideways, which probably led to other workings of the big mines.

'If we don't keep to this main road, we'll lose ourselves,' said Philip, and Lucy-Ann gave a gasp. It had not occurred to her that they might get lost. How awful to go wandering about miles of mine-workings, and never find the shaft that led them upwards!

They came to a place where, quite suddenly, a brilliant light shone. The children had rounded a corner, noticing, as they came to it, that a glimmer of light seemed to show there. As they turned the corner of the passage they came into a cave lighted by a powerful lamp. They stopped in the greatest surprise.

Then a noise came to their ears – a queer noise, not the muffled boom of the sea, but a clattering noise that they couldn't recognise – then a bang, then a clattering noise again.

'We've found where the miners work,' said Jack, in an excited whisper. 'Keep back a bit. We may see them – but we don't want them to see us!'

20

Prisoners Underground

The children huddled against the wall, trying to see what was in the cave before them, blinking their eyes in the brilliant light.

There were boxes and crates in the cave, but nothing else. No man was there. But in the near distance was somebody at work, making that queer clattering, banging noise.

'Let's go back,' said Lucy-Ann, frightened.

'No. But look – there's a passage going off just here,' whispered Philip, flashing his torch into a dark tunnel. 'We'll creep down there and see if we come across the miners working somewhere near.'

So they all crept down the tunnel. As they went down it, pressing themselves closely against the rocky sides, a rock fell from the roof. It gave Kiki such a fright that she gave a squawk and flew off Jack's shoulder.

'Here, Kiki!' said Jack, afraid of losing her. But Kiki did not come back to his shoulder. The boy stumbled back up the passage to look for her, whistling softly in the way he did when he wanted to call her to him. The others did not realise that he was no longer with them, but went on down the tunnel, slowly and painfully.

And then things happened very quickly. Someone came swiftly up the tunnel with a lantern, whose light picked out the three children at once. They cowered back against the wall and tried not to be dazzled by the lantern. The man carrying it paused in the greatest astonishment.

'Well,' he said, in a deep, rather hoarse voice. 'Well – if this doesn't beat everything!' He held his lantern up high to see the children more clearly. Then he called over his shoulder.

'Jake! Come and take a look-see here. I've got something here that'll make your eyes drop out.'

Another man came swiftly up, tall and dark in the shadows. He gave a loud exclamation as he saw the three children.

'Well, what do you think of that!' he said. 'Children! How did *they* come here? Are they real? Or am I dreaming?'

'It's children all right,' said the first man. He spoke to the three, and his voice was rough and harsh.

'What are you doing here? Who are you with?'

'We're by ourselves,' said Philip.

The man laughed loudly. 'Oh no, you're not.

It's no good spinning that kind of tale to us. Who brought you here, and why?'

'We came ourselves in a boat,' said Lucy-Ann indignantly. 'We know the gap in the rocks, and we came to see the island.'

'Why did you come down here?' demanded Jake, coming nearer. Now the children could see what he was like, and they didn't like the look of him at all. He had a black patch over one eye, and the other eye gleamed wickedly at them. His mouth was so tight-lipped that it almost seemed as if he had no lips at all. Lucy-Ann cowered away.

'Go on – why did you come down here?' demanded Jake.

'Well – we found the shaft hole – and we climbed down to see the old mines,' said Philip. 'We shan't split on you, don't be afraid.'

'Split on us? What do you mean? What do you know, boy?' asked Jake roughly.

Philip said nothing. He didn't really know what to say. Jake nodded his head to the first man, who went behind the children. Now they could not go forwards or backwards to escape.

Lucy-Ann began to cry. Philip put his arm round her, and wondered, for the first time, where Jack was. Lucy-Ann looked round for him too. She began to cry more loudly when she saw he was not there.

'Lucy-Ann, don't tell these men that Jack is gone,' whispered Philip. 'If they take us prisoner, Jack will be able to escape and bring help. So don't say a word about him.'

'What are you whispering about?' asked Jake. 'Now, look here, my boy – you don't want any harm to come to your sisters, do you? Well – you just tell us what you know, and maybe we'll let you go.'

Philip was alarmed at the man's tone. For the first time it dawned on the boy that there might be danger. These men were fierce – they wouldn't let three children share their secrets willingly. Suppose they kept them prisoner underground – starved them – beat them? Who knew what might happen? Philip made up his mind to tell a little of what he guessed.

'Look here,' he said to Jake, 'we know who you

are working with, see? And he's a friend of ours. He'll be mighty angry if you do us any harm.'

'Oh, really!' said Jake, in a mocking tone. 'And who is this wonderful friend of yours?'

'Bill Smugs,' said Philip, feeling certain that everything would be all right at the mention of Bill's name.

'Bill Smugs?' said the man, with a jeering note in his voice. 'And who may *he* be? I've never heard of him in my life.'

'But you must have,' said Philip desperately. 'He brings you food, and signals to you. You know he does. You *must* know Bill Smugs and his boat, *The Albatross.*'

The two men stared intently at the children. Then they spoke together quickly in a foreign language. They seemed puzzled.

'Bill Smugs is no friend of ours,' Jake said, after a pause. 'Did he tell you that he knew us?'

'Oh no,' said Philip. 'We only guessed it.'

'Then you guessed wrong,' said the man. 'Come along – we're going to make you comfortable somewhere till we decide what to do with children who poke their noses into things that don't concern them.'

Philip guessed that they were going to be kept prisoners somewhere underground, and he was alarmed and angry. The girls were frightened. Dinah didn't cry, but Lucy-Ann, forlorn because Jack was not by her, cried without stopping.

Jake prodded Philip to make him go along in front of him. He turned the children off into a narrow passage running at right angles from the tunnel they were in. A door was set across this passage and Jake unbolted it. He pushed the children inside the cave there, which looked almost like a small room, for it had benches and a small table. Jake set his lantern down on the table.

'You'll be safe here,' he said, with a horrid crooked grin. 'Quite safe. I shan't starve you, don't be afraid of that.'

The children were left alone. They heard the door bolted firmly and footsteps dying away. Lucy-Ann still wept.

'What a bit of bad luck!' said Philip, trying to speak cheerfully. 'Don't cry, Lucy-Ann.'

'Why didn't those men know Bill Smugs?' said Dinah, puzzled. 'We know he must bring them food, and probably take away the copper they mine.'

'Easy to guess,' said Philip gloomily. 'I bet old Bill gave us a wrong name. It sounds pretty peculiar, anyway – Bill *Smugs* – I never heard a name like that before, now I come to think of it.'

'Oh – you think it isn't his real name?' said Dinah. 'So of course those men don't know it. Dash! If only we knew his real name, everything would be all right.'

'What are we going to do?' wept Lucy-Ann. 'I don't like being a prisoner in a copper mine under the sea. It's horrid.'

'But it's a very thrilling adventure, Lucy-Ann,' said Philip, trying to comfort her.

'I don't like a thrilling adventure when I'm in the middle of it,' wept Lucy-Ann. Neither did the others, very much. Philip wondered about Jack.

'What can have happened to him?' he said.

'I hope he's safe. He'll be able to rescue us if he is.'

But at that moment Jack was anything but safe. He had wandered up the tunnel looking for Kiki, had turned into another passage, found Kiki, turned to go back – and then had lost his way. He had no idea that the others had been caught. Kiki was on his shoulder, talking softly to herself.

Philip had the map, not Jack. So, once the boy had lost his way, he had no means of discovering how to get back to the main passage. He turned into one tunnel after another, found some of them blocked, turned back, and began wandering helplessly here and there.

'Kiki, we're lost,' said Jack. He shouted again and again, as loudly as he could, and his voice went echoing through the ancient tunnels very weirdly, coming back to him time and time again. Kiki screeched too, but there was no answering call.

The children shut up in the cell-like cave fell silent after a time. There was nothing to do, nothing to say. Lucy-Ann put her head down on her arms, which she rested on the table, and fell fast asleep, tired out. Dinah and Philip stretched themselves out on the benches and tried to sleep too. But they couldn't.

'Philip, we'll just *have* to escape from here,' said Dinah desperately.

'Easy to say that,' said Philip sarcastically. 'Not so easy to do. How would you suggest that we escape from a cave set deep in a copper mine under the sea, a cave which has a stout wooden door to it well bolted on the outside? Don't be foolish.'

'I've got an idea, Philip,' said Dinah at last. Philip grunted. Dinah's ideas were rather farfetched as a rule.

'Now, do listen, Philip,' said Dinah earnestly. 'It's quite a good idea.'

'What is it?' said Philip grumpily.

'Well, Jake or that other man will be sure to come back here sooner or later with food,' began Dinah. 'And when he comes, let's all be gasping and holding our breaths and groaning.'

'Whatever for?' asked Philip in astonishment.

'So as to make him think the air is very bad in

here, and we can't breathe, and we're almost dying,' said Dinah. 'Then maybe he'll let us go out into the passage for a breath of air – and you can reel towards him, kick out his light – and we'll all escape as quickly as we can.'

Philip sat up and looked at his sister with admiration. 'I really do think you've got an idea there,' he said, and Dinah glowed with pleasure. 'Yes, I really do. We'll have to wake Lucy-Ann and tell her. She must play her part too.'

So Lucy-Ann was awakened and told the plan. She thought it was very good. She began to gasp and hold her head and moan in a most realistic way. Philip nodded his head.

'That's fine,' he said. 'We'll all do that when we hear Jake or the other fellow coming. Now, whilst there's still time, I'd better find where we are on the underground map, and see exactly what direction to take as soon as we've kicked the man's light out.'

He spread the map out on the table and studied it. 'Yes,' he said at last. 'I see where we are. There's the big cave that was lighted up – see? And the little passage off it where we were caught – and here's the passage we were taken down – and here's the little cave we're in now. Now, listen, girls – as soon as I've kicked out the man's light, take my hand and keep close by me. I'll lead you the right way, and find the shaft-hole again. Then up we'll go, join up with old Jack somewhere, and get to the boat.'

'Good,' said Dinah, thrilled – and at that very moment they heard footsteps coming to the wooden door.

21

Escape – But What About Jack?

The bolts were shot back. The door opened and Jake appeared, carrying a tin plate of biscuits, and a big open tin of sardines. He also put on the table a jug of water.

Then he stared in amazement at the three children. Philip seemed to be choking, and he rolled off his bench on the floor. Dinah was making the most extraordinary noises, and holding her head tightly in her hands. Lucy-Ann appeared to be on the point of being sick, and made the most alarming groans.

'What's up?' asked Jake.

'Air! We want air!' gasped Philip. 'We're choking! Air! Air!'

Dinah rolled on to the ground as well. Jake pulled her up and hustled her to the door. He pushed the others out into the passage. He thought they must really be on the point of choking – the air in the cell must be used up.

Philip watched his chance and reeled towards Jake as if he could not stand straight. As he came towards him he lifted his right foot, and aimed a mighty kick at the lantern in Jake's hand. It fell and smashed at once, and the light went out. There was a tinkling of glass, a shout from Jake – and then Philip sought for the hands of the two frightened girls. He found them and pushed the two hurriedly in front of him towards a passage on the left. Jake, left in the darkness, began to grope about, shouting for the other man.

'Olly! Hi, Olly! Bring a lamp! Quick! These dratted kids have fooled me. Hi, *Olly!*'

Philip, trying hard to keep his sense of direction correct, hurried the girls along. Their hearts were beating painfully, and Lucy-Ann really did feel as if she was going to choke now. Soon they had left Jake's shouts behind and were in the wide main passage down which they had come not many hours before. Philip was now using his torch, and it was

pleasant to see the thin, bright beam of light.

'Thank goodness – we're in the right tunnel,' said Philip, pausing to listen. He could hear nothing but the boom of the sea far above their heads. He swung his torch around. Yes – they were on the right road. Good!

'Can we have a little rest?' panted Lucy-Ann.

'No,' said Philip. 'Those men will be after us almost at once – as soon as they get another lamp. They will guess we are making for the shaft. Come on. There's no time to be lost.'

The children hurried on again – but after a time, to their great dismay, they heard shouts behind them. That meant that the men were after them – and what was more, were catching them up. Lucy-Ann felt so alarmed that she could hardly run.

They came at last to the big shaft-hole. It was so deep that the children could not see the entrance to it, far above. The daylight was not to be seen.

'Up you go,' said Philip anxiously. 'You first, Lucy-Ann. Be as quick as you can.'

Lucy-Ann began to climb. Dinah followed her,

Philip came last. He could hear the men's voices even more clearly now. And then – quite suddenly, they stopped, and Philip could hear them no more. What had happened?

An extraordinary thing had happened. Kiki the parrot, hearing the tumult in the distance, had become excited and was shouting. She and Jack were still wandering about, quite lost, in the maze of passages and galleries. Kiki's sharp ears heard the men and she began to screech and yell.

'Wipe your feet! Shut the door! Hi, hi, hi, Polly put the kettle on!'

The men heard the shouting voice and thought it belonged to the children. 'They've lost themselves,' said Jake, stopping. 'They don't know the way back to the shaft. They're lost and are shouting for help.'

'Let them shout,' said Olly sourly. 'They'll never find the way to the shaft. I told you they wouldn't. Let them get lost and starve.'

'No,' said Jake. 'We can't do that. We don't want to have to explain half-starving children to search-parties, do we? We'd better go and get them. They are over in that direction.'

They went off the main passage, meaning to try and find the children where the shouts had come from. Kiki's voice came again to them. 'Wipe your feet, idiot, wipe your feet!'

This astonished the two men. They went on towards the voice, but even as they went, Jack and Kiki wandered into a passage that the two men missed. Kiki fell silent, and the men paused.

'Can't hear them any more,' said Jake. 'Better go to the shaft. They may have found their way there after all. We can't afford to let them escape till we've decided what to do about all this.'

So they retraced their steps to the shaft, and looked up it. A shower of stones came down and hit them.

'Gosh! The children *are* up there!' cried Jake, and started up the ladder at once.

The children were almost at the top. Lucy-Ann felt as if her arms and legs could not climb one more rung – but they held out, and at last the tired girl reached the top, climbed out, and rolled over on the ground, exhausted. Dinah came next, and sat down with a long sigh. And then Philip, tired too, but determined not to rest for one moment.

'I'm sure those men will come up the shaft after us,' he said. 'We haven't a minute to lose. Do come on, girls. We must get to the boat and be off before anyone stops us.'

It was getting dark. What a long time they must have been underground! Philip dragged the girls to their feet and they set off to the shore. The boat was there, thank goodness.

'I don't want to go without Jack,' said Lucy-Ann obstinately, her heart wrung with anxiety for her beloved brother. But Philip bundled her into the boat at once.

'No time to lose,' he said. 'Come on. We'll send

help back for Jack as soon as ever we can. I can't bear leaving him behind either – but I've got to get you girls away safely.'

Dinah took one pair of oars and Philip the other. Soon the two were rowing the boat away quickly, across the calm channel of water to where, in the distance, the waves thundered over the reef of rocks. Philip felt anxious. It was one thing to get through the gap safely when he could see where he was going, but quite another when it was almost dark.

He heard shouting, but he was too far away from the shore to see the men there. Jake and Olly had climbed up the shaft, raced over the island to the shore, and were looking for a boat. But there was none. The tide was coming in and there was not even a mark on the sand to show where the boat had rested. In fact, it had been almost afloat when the children had got in, and it was lucky that it had not floated away.

'No boat here,' said Olly. 'How did those kids come? It's strange. They *must* have escaped by boat.

They can't still be underground. We'd better signal tonight and get someone over here. We must warn them that kids have found us underground.'

They went back to the shaft and climbed down it, not knowing that one of the children was still wandering about in the mines. Poor Jack was still making his way down a maze of tunnels, all looking exactly alike to him.

In the meantime Philip, Lucy-Ann and Dinah had, by great good luck, just struck the gap in the rocks. It was really because of Lucy-Ann's sharp ears that they had been so lucky. She had listened to the pounding of the water over the rocks, and her ears had noticed a softening of the thunder. 'That's where the gap must be,' she thought. 'The noise dies away a little there.' So, sitting at the tiller, she tried to guide the boat to where she guessed the gap to be, and by good chance she found it. The boat slipped through, scraping its keel once more on the rock just below the surface – and then it was in the open sea, rocking up and down.

How Philip put up the sail in the half darkness,

and sailed the boat home, he never quite knew. He was desperate; they must get back safely, so with great courage he went about his task. When at last he reached the mooring-place, under the cliff, he could not get out of the boat. Quite suddenly his knees seemed to give way, and he could not walk.

'I'll have to wait a minute or two,' he said to Dinah. 'My legs have gone funny. I'll be all right soon.'

'You've been awfully clever,' said Dinah, and from her those words meant a lot.

They tied up the boat at last and went up to the house. Aunt Polly met them at the door, in a great state of alarm.

'Wherever have you been? I've been so worried about you. I've been nearly off my head with anxiety. I really feel faint.'

She looked very white and ill. Even as she spoke, she tottered a little, and Philip bounded forward and caught her as she fell.

'Poor Aunt Polly,' he said, dragging her indoors as gently as he could and putting her on the sofa.

'We're so sorry we upset you. I'll get some water –
no, Dinah, you get some.'

Soon Aunt Polly said she felt a little better, but
it was quite plain that she was ill. 'She never could
stand any worry of this sort,' Dinah said to Lucy-
Ann. 'Once Philip nearly fell down the cliff, she was
ill for days. It seems to make her heart bad. I'll get
her to bed.'

'Don't say a word about Jack being missing,'
Philip warned Dinah in a low voice. 'That really will
give her a heart attack.'

Dinah went off upstairs with her aunt, supporting
her as firmly as she could. Philip went to look for
Joe. He wasn't back yet. Good! Then he wouldn't
have missed the boat. He looked at Lucy-Ann's
white little face, its green tired eyes and worried
expression. He felt sorry for her.

'What are we going to do about Jack?' said
Lucy-Ann, with a gulp. 'We've got to rescue him,
Philip.'

'I know,' said Philip. 'Well – we can't tell Aunt
Polly – and Uncle Jocelyn wouldn't be any good –

and we'd be idiots to tell Joe. So there is no one left but Bill, I'm afraid.'

'But – you said we'd better not tell Bill we knew his secret,' said Lucy-Ann.

'I know. But we've got to, now that Jack is alone on the island,' said Philip. 'Bill will have to go and tell those fierce friends of his that Jack is a pal, and he'll find him and bring him back safely. So don't worry, Lucy-Ann.'

'Will you go and tell him now, straight away?' asked Lucy-Ann tearfully.

'I'll go just as soon as ever I've had something to eat,' said Philip, suddenly feeling so hungry that he felt he could eat a whole loaf, a pound of butter, and a jar of jam. 'You'd better have something too, Lucy-Ann – you look as white as a sheet. Cheer up! Jack will soon be safe here, and we'll all be laughing and talking like anything.'

Dinah came down then, and set about getting some food. They all very hungry, even Lucy-Ann. Dinah agreed that the only thing to do was to go to Bill Smugs and get him to go and rescue Jack before the men found him.

'They'll be so wild that we've escaped that they may be really tough with Jack,' said Dinah, and then wished she hadn't spoken the words, for Lucy-Ann looked scared to death.

'Please go, Philip,' begged the little girl. 'Go now. If you don't, I shall.'

'Don't be silly,' said Philip, getting up. 'You don't want to make your way across the cliff on a dark night. You'd fall over the edge! Well – so long! I'll be back.'

Off went the boy, climbing the steep path to the top of the cliff. Then he set off to find Bill. He saw the lights of Joe's car in the distance, coming home, and heard the noise of the engine. He hurried so that he would not be seen.

'Bill *will* be surprised to see me,' he thought. 'He'll wonder whoever it is, knocking at his door in the middle of the night.'

But alas – Bill wasn't there when Philip at last arrived at the shack. *Now* what was he to do?

22

A Talk with Bill – and a Shock

Philip was filled with dismay. It had never occurred to him that Bill might not be at home. How awful! Philip sat down on a stool and tried to think – but he was tired out, and his brain wouldn't seem to work.

'What shall I do now? What shall I do now?' he thought, and could not seem to think of anything else. 'What shall I do now?'

It was dark in the little shack. Philip sat on the stool, his hands hanging limply between his legs. Then he became aware of something at the back of the shack, and he turned to see what it was.

To his great amazement he saw a red light there, glowing deeply. Then it disappeared. Then it came back again, went out, reappeared. It went on doing this for a few minutes, whilst Philip tried to think what it was, and why it seemed to be signalling. At

last he got up and went over to the light. It came from a small bulb beside the radio. Philip had a look at it. He twiddled one or two knobs. A Morse code came from it when he twiddled another. Then by chance he saw, at the back of the set, a small telephone receiver, smaller than any he had seen before – almost a pocket size, he thought.

He picked it up – and immediately he heard a voice crackling in the receiver. He lifted it to his ear.

'Y2 calling,' said the voice. 'Y2. Y2 calling.'

Philip listened in, astonished. He decided to speak to the voice.

'Hallo!' he said. 'Who are you?'

There was a moment's silence. Evidently Y2, whoever he might be, was surprised. A cautious voice came over the phone again.

'Who is there?'

'A boy called Philip Mannering,' said Philip. 'I came to find Bill Smugs, but he isn't here.'

'Who did you say?' said the voice.

'Bill Smugs. But he's not here,' repeated Philip. 'I say, who are you? Do you want me to leave a message for Bill? I expect he'll be back some time.'

'How long has he been gone?' asked Y2.

'Don't know,' said Philip. 'Wait – I can hear someone. Here he comes, I do believe.'

Joyfully the boy put down the tiny telephone receiver. He had heard the low sound of whistling outside, and footsteps. It must be Bill.

It was. He came in, shining his torch – and he was so surprised when he saw Philip there that he stood stock-still without saying a word.

'Oh, Bill!' said Philip happily. 'I'm so glad you've come. Quick! – somebody wants you on the phone – Y2 he says he is.'

'Did you speak to him?' said Bill, his voice sounding astonished. He picked up the tiny phone and spoke curtly.

'Is that Y2? L4 speaking.'

The voice evidently asked him who Philip was.

'Boy that lives round here,' said Bill. 'What's the news, please?'

Then all that was said by Bill was 'Yes. Of course. I'll let you know. Thanks. No, nothing yet. Goodbye.'

He turned to Philip when he had finished talking. 'Look here, my boy,' he said, 'please understand that if you come paying calls here when I am out, you must on no account tamper with my possessions or meddle with my affairs.'

Bill had never spoken so sternly before, and Philip's heart sank. What would Bill say when he knew that the children had guessed his secret? He would think they had been meddling more than ever.

'Sorry, Bill,' he said awkwardly. 'I didn't mean to interfere at all.'

'Why have you come at this time of night?' asked Bill.

'Bill – is this your pencil?' asked Philip, taking it out. He hoped that when Bill saw it he would remember that he had dropped it down in the copper mines, and would guess, without Philip saying any more, that the children knew his secret. Bill stared at the yellow pencil stub.

'Yes, that's mine,' he said. 'But you didn't come here at night to give me back my pencil. What have you come for?'

'Oh, Bill – don't be so cross,' said poor Philip. 'You see – we know your secret. We know what you are doing here. We know why you go to the island – we know everything.'

Bill listened to all this as if he simply could not believe his ears. He stared at Philip in the utmost amazement. His eyes grew narrow, and his mouth hardened into a thin line. For a moment he looked very frightening.

'You are going to tell me exactly what you mean by all this,' said Bill, in a horrid sort of voice. 'What *is* my secret? What is the "everything" that you know?'

'Well,' said Philip desperately, 'we know that you and your friends are trying to work the copper mines again – and we know that you are here, with your boat and your car, to provide them with food – and to take away any copper they find. We know you've been down the mines, visiting the men there. We know you've given us a false name. But, please, Bill, we wouldn't dream of giving you away – we hope you'll get lots of copper.'

Bill listened, his eyes still narrow – but as Philip went on talking, the twinkle came back into them, and his mouth looked like Bill's again.

'Well, well, well – so you know all that,' said Bill. 'And what else do you know? How did you get to the island? Not in my boat, I hope?'

'Oh no,' said Philip, relieved to see Bill looking friendly again. 'We took Joe's when he was out. We went right down into the mines too – that was where we found your pencil. But we don't like your friends there, Bill. They took us prisoner – they're horrid – and even when we mentioned your name to them and said we were friends of yours, they said they didn't know it and wouldn't let us go free.'

'You told them you knew Bill Smugs?' said Bill. Philip nodded.

'What men did you see?' asked Bill. His voice had become sharp again, and he snapped out his questions in rather a frightening manner.

'Two – one called Jake and one Olly,' said Philip. Bill made a note in his notebook. 'What were they like?' he asked sharply.

'Well – but you must know them,' said Philip in astonishment. 'Anyway, I couldn't really see much – either it was dark – or the light dazzled me. I just saw that Jake was tall and dark, with a patch over one eye, that's all. But you must know what they are like yourself, Bill.'

'See anyone or anything else?' asked Bill.

Philip shook his head. 'No. We heard other miners at work, though – a terrific clattering, banging sort of noise, you know – they must have found some part of the mine that was still rich in copper. Bill, are you finding much copper there? Will it make you rich?'

'Look here, you didn't come here tonight to tell me all this,' said Bill suddenly. 'What *did* you come for?'

'I came to say that although Dinah and Lucy-Ann and I managed to fool Jake and get away – we had to leave Jack behind – with Kiki,' said Philip. 'And we are worried about him. You see, he might get lost for ever in those workings under the sea – or those friends of yours might find him and ill-treat him because they are angry at our tricking them as we did.'

'Jack's still there – on the island – in the mines!' said Bill, looking quite shocked. 'Good heavens! This is serious. Why didn't you tell me that at first? My word, it looks as if everything's going to be ruined by you kids.'

Bill looked angry and upset. He went to his radio, fiddled about with the knobs, and then, to Philip's amazement, began to talk in short, sharp tones, in a language the boy did not know.

'It's a transmitter as well as a receiving set,' thought Philip. 'This is all very mysterious. Who is Bill talking to now? Have they all got a boss who is directing this copper mine affair? I suppose there's very big money in it. Oh dear, I hope we haven't really ruined things for them. What does Bill mean? How could we have spoilt anything? He's only got to go over to the island, see his friends, tell them to set Jack free, and that would finish it. He might know he can trust us not to split on him.'

Bill turned round. 'We must get the boat at once,' he said. 'Come on.'

With their torches throwing beams of light before them they went down to where the boat was kept. Bill began to push it out – and then he suddenly gave such a shout that Philip's heart nearly jumped out of his body.

'Who's done that?'

Bill shone his torch into the boat – and Philip saw, with a shock of dismay and fear, that someone had chopped viciously at the bottom of the boat – chopped so hard that there were holes there through

which the water was even now pouring.

Bill pulled her back on the beach again, his face very grim. 'Do you know anything about that?' he asked Philip.

'Of course not,' said the boy. 'Golly – who did it, Bill? This is awful.'

'Well – the boat is no use at all till she's repaired,' said Bill. 'But somehow we've got to get over to the Isle of Gloom. We'll have to take Joe's boat. Come on. But mind – he mustn't know a thing about it. There's too much known about everything already – and too many people nosing about for my liking.'

They set off over the cliffs, poor Philip so tired that he could hardly keep up with Bill. They came to Craggy-Tops, climbed down the cliff path and made their way to where Joe's boat was always tied.

But, to their intense surprise and despair, Joe's boat was not there. It was gone.

23

Another Secret Passage

After Philip had left, Lucy-Ann and Dinah tried to settle down to some sewing. But Lucy-Ann's hands trembled so much that she kept pricking her finger.

'I'd better go and tell Uncle Jocelyn that Aunt Polly has gone to bed, feeling ill,' said Dinah. 'Come with me, Lucy-Ann.'

The two girls went off to the study and knocked at the door. They went in, and Dinah told her uncle about her aunt. He nodded, hardly seeming to hear.

'Uncle Jocelyn,' said Dinah, 'have you any more maps of the Isle of Gloom? Or any books about it?'

'No,' said her uncle. 'But wait – there's a book about this house, Craggy-Tops, I think. You know that it was a great place for illegal goings-on and secret doings two or three hundred years ago? I believe there was a secret passage to it from the beach.'

'Yes, there is,' said Dinah. 'We know it.'

Her uncle became quite excited. He made her tell him all about it. 'Dear me,' he said, 'I thought it had fallen in long ago. But these secret passages hewn out of the rock last for years. Still, I should think the one that goes under the sea to the Isle of Gloom has been flooded long since.'

The two girls stared at the old man in amazement. Dinah found her tongue at last.

'Uncle Jocelyn, do you mean to say there was another secret passage here – under the sea to the island? Why, it's ever so far away!'

'Well, there was supposed to be,' said her uncle. 'There's something about it in that book. Now – where is it?'

The girls waited in the greatest impatience whilst he found the book. He put his hand on it at last and Dinah almost snatched it from him.

'Thank you, Uncle,' she said, and before he could say she must not take it out of the room, she and Lucy-Ann rushed out of the door and sped to the sitting-room as fast as they could. *Another passage* . . . this time to the island itself ! What a thrill! Surely Uncle Jocelyn must be mistaken.

'It's quite likely it's true, though,' said Dinah excitedly. 'I know this whole coast is honeycombed with caves and passages – it's noted for that. Some districts are, you know, Lucy-Ann. I expect the passage joins up with the mine-workings that extend right under the sea-bed. We know there are miles of them.'

The girls opened the funny old book. They could not read the printing, partly because it was so faded and partly because the letters were shaped differently from the ones they knew. They turned over page after page, looking for maps or pictures.

The book was apparently a history of Craggy-Tops, which was hundreds of years old. In those days it must have been almost a castle, built securely on the cliff rock, protected by the sea in front, and the cliff behind. Now, of course, it was half ruined, and the family lived only in the few rooms that were still habitable.

'Look,' said Dinah, pointing to a queer old map,

'that's what Craggy-Tops was like in the old days. What a fine place! Look at the towers – and what a grand front it had!'

They turned over the pages. They came to one that had a kind of diagram on it. The girls studied it closely. Then Lucy-Ann gave a shout. 'I know what this is – it's the secret passage from the cellar to the beach. Isn't it?'

It was. There was no doubt about that. The girls felt excited. Perhaps the book would show the other passage too.

There were two or three more diagram-like maps, some of them so faded that it was impossible to see what they were meant to represent. Dinah gave a sigh.

'I wish I could read this old printing. If I could, I might be able to find out whether any of these maps are meant to show the other secret passage – the one to the island. It would be so exciting to discover that. What a thrill if we did! What will the boys say when we tell them there's actually a way to the island under the sea itself?'

That made Lucy-Ann think of Jack, and her face clouded over. Where was Jack? Had Philip got Bill Smugs to go out in his boat and rescue him? Were they even now bringing Jack safely back again?

As she thought about this, she heard Philip's voice in the passage outside the sitting-room. She jumped up in delight. Had Philip and Bill brought back Jack already? How marvellously quick they had been! She ran to the door joyfully.

But outside there were only Bill and Philip – no Jack. Lucy-Ann called out to them.

'Where's Jack? Haven't you rescued him? Where is he?'

'Bill's boat has been smashed up by someone,' said Philip, going into the room. 'So we came to get Joe's. And that's gone too. I suppose Joe is doing some of his usual night fishing. So we're stumped – don't know what to do.'

The girls stared at the two in dismay. No boat – no way of rescuing poor Jack? Lucy-Ann's eyes filled with tears as she thought of Jack lost in those dark endless caves, with those fierce men ready to catch him and imprison him. She felt glad he had Kiki with him.

'Oh, Philip,' said Dinah, suddenly remembering, 'do you know what Uncle Jocelyn told us tonight? He said there used to be a way under the sea to the copper mines – to the island! He knew about the other secret passage, but he didn't think it was still usable. He was surprised. Oh, Philip, do you suppose the secret passage to the island is still there? Do you think it has been flooded by the sea – or fallen in? Oh, how I wish we could find it!'

Bill looked suddenly interested. He picked up the book Dinah held. 'This is a book about the old house?' he asked. Dinah nodded.

'Yes – our own secret passage is in it, the one we found ourselves – and I expect the other is too, only we can't understand the old maps and the printing.'

'Well, I can,' said Bill, and became lost in the book, turning over the pages slowly, skipping a few here and there, looking for details of the way to the Isle of Gloom.

He suddenly began to look excited, and turned

over one or two pages very quickly. He looked hard at first one queer map and then another. Then he asked a peculiar question.

'How deep is your well here?'

'The well?' said Philip, in amazement. 'Ooooh – awfully deep – deep as the shaft-hole in the island, I should think. It goes down below sea level, anyway, but there's not a trace of salt in it, of course.'

'Look here,' said Bill, and spelt out a few words in the book to make them clear to the children, and then he turned to a map. It showed a deep shaft going down into the earth. 'See?' said Bill. 'The beginning of the passage to the island is down at the bottom of your well. It's quite obvious that that would be the place, anyway, if I'd thought about it – you see, to go under the sea-bed to the mines means that the entrance must be below sea level – and that's the only spot here below sea level – the well, of course!'

'Gosh!' said all three children at once. The well! They hadn't thought of that. How extraordinary!

'But – there's water at the bottom of the well,'

said Philip. 'You can't go through the water, surely.'

'No – look,' said Bill Smugs, and he pointed to the map. 'The entrance to the passage is above the water-line of the well. See? These must be steps, I should think, cut in an opening of the shaft, leading upwards a little way, and then through a passage in the rock itself – a natural crack, I imagine, such as this coast is full of – which someone discovered, followed up, and by means of pickaxes or blasting, made into a usable passage.'

'I see,' said Philip excitedly. 'I suppose when they sank the shaft for the well, someone discovered the hole deep down, explored it, found it was a sort of natural passage, and, as you say, followed it up, and made use of it. Bill – could we get down there and find out?'

'Not now, in the middle of the night,' said Bill at once. 'You've all had enough adventure for this one day – we must go to bed.'

'But – but what about Jack?' asked Lucy-Ann, her green eyes wide with anxiety.

'We can't do anything about him tonight,' said

Bill, firmly but kindly. 'Anyway, if he's caught, he's caught, and if he's not, we may be able to do something about him tomorrow. But we are *not* going to go down wells in buckets in the dead of night, so that's that. Philip, I'll sleep with you in the tower-room tonight.'

Philip was glad. He did not want to sleep alone that night. The girls were sent off to bed, in spite of their protests that they were not tired, and Philip and Bill climbed the spiral stairway to the little tower-room. Philip showed Bill the window from which they could see the island at times.

Then he sat down on the bed to take off his shoes. But he was so tired that even the effort of undoing the laces was too much for him. He rolled over on the bed, shut his eyes, and fell fast asleep, fully dressed as he was. Bill looked at him and smiled. He drew a cover over him, and sat at the window to think.

Tomorrow would show whether or not there was still a way from Craggy-Tops to the island. Bill felt certain there would not be. True, the other passage was still usable, but that was very short compared with the other – and this second one had had the sea pounding on top of it for many, many years. A crack in it – a trickle of water down – and the passage would be flooded in a very few weeks. Then it would be impassable.

Bill went to bed at last, stretched himself out beside the sleeping boy, and fell asleep himself. He was awakened by Philip, who was shaking him.

'Bill! It's morning! Let's have breakfast and try and find that well passage. Hurry!'

They were soon downstairs, to find the girls there, already cooking bacon and eggs for breakfast. 'Where's Joe?' asked Philip, in surprise.

'Hasn't come back from fishing yet,' said Dinah, getting a fried egg deftly out of the pan. 'Here you are, Bill. I'll do an egg for you now, Philip. It's a good thing Joe isn't back, isn't it? – or he'd wonder what on earth Bill was doing here. He would think it all mighty suspicious.'

'Joe may be back at any minute,' said Lucy-Ann. 'So let's hurry before he comes. I'd just hate him to stand glowering at the head of the well whilst we explore it all that way below.'

They finished their breakfast quickly. Dinah had already taken some to her aunt in her bedroom, and to her uncle in his study. She said Aunt Polly was feeling a bit better and would be down later. She didn't think Uncle Jocelyn had gone to bed at all.

'I really believe he works all night long,' said Dinah. 'Now – have we all finished? I'll leave the washing-up till I get back.'

They all went out into the little yard that lay behind the house, backing on to the sheer rise of the cliff. Bill leaned over the well. It certainly was very, very deep.

'Do we go down in the bucket?' asked Philip.

'We could if there was a really big one,' said Dinah. 'But we can't possibly go down in this. Not even Lucy-Ann could get into it.'

'You know,' said Bill, taking his big torch from his pocket. 'You know, if this well-shaft is really the only way down to the entrance of the island passage, there should be a ladder. I can't imagine

people going up and down in buckets.'

'Well – there isn't a ladder,' said Philip. 'I should have seen it if there was.'

Bill flashed his torch down the well, examining the sides carefully. 'Look,' he said to Philip, 'it is true there is no ladder – but do you see those iron staples jutting out from the wall down there? Well, those are what would be used to help anyone wanting to descend this well-hole. They would use them as steps, holding on to the ones above with their hands, and going down bit by bit – feeling with their feet for the next one.'

'Yes!' said Philip, in excitement. 'You're right! That's the way that people went down in the olden days. I bet when there was fighting round about here, many refugees used this old well as a hiding-place, even if they didn't know of the passage entrance down below. Come on, Bill – let's go down. I'm simply longing to get going.'

'Well, it's time we did,' said Bill. 'I'll go first. Keep a watch out for Joe, Dinah.'

24

A Journey Under the Sea

Bill couldn't reach the first iron staples, so Philip had to fetch a rope. It was tied tightly to an iron post by the well, and then Bill slipped down it, and placed his feet on the first staples.

'I'm all right,' he said. 'You come along as soon as you can, Philip – let me get down a few steps first – and for goodness' sake don't slip.'

The girls did not go – and, indeed, neither of them liked the thought of going down the steep, cold well-shaft with only insecure staples for a foot- and hand-hold. They watched the two disappearing down into the dark, and shivered.

'It's beastly to be left behind, but I honestly think it's beastlier to go down there,' said Dinah. 'Come on – we can't see or hear Bill and Philip now – we'd better go back to the kitchen and do a few jobs. Isn't Joe late!'

They went back, wondering how Bill and Philip were getting on down the well. They were climbing down slowly but surely; the staples seemed to be as firmly in the wall as when they were first driven in.

It was tiring work, and would have been utterly impossible to tackle if it had not been for unexpected resting-places let into the well-wall every now and again. The first one puzzled Bill, till he guessed what it was. It was an opening in the well-wall, going back a few feet, big enough to crouch in and rest. At first Bill had half thought the first one to be the entrance to the passage and he was surprised to come to it so soon. But he quickly realised what it was, and very thankfully he rested there a few minutes. Then Philip had a rest there, whilst Bill went slowly downwards, his feet always feeling for the next staple.

It seemed ages going down the well-shaft, and, in fact it took the two of them nearly an hour. They used each resting-place, but in spite of that they became very tired. Then suddenly Bill's torch, which he had stuck into his belt alight, gleamed on to dark water. They were at the bottom.

'We're there!' Bill yelled up to Philip. 'I'm just going to look about for the entrance.'

It was easy to find, for there, in the well-wall, was a round, gaping hole like a small tunnel. Bill slipped into it. It was dark, slimy, and evil-smelling. 'Funny that the air is still fresh,' thought Bill. 'But all the way down the well I could feel a current of air blowing round me – so there must be some sort of through-draught to keep it pure.'

He waited for Philip. Then the two of them set out on what must surely have been one of the strangest roads in the world – a path under the bed of the sea itself. At first the tunnel was narrow and led upwards a little by means of steps, and the two had to crouch down to get along. But after a bit it widened out and became higher. It was still slimy and evil-smelling, but they got used to that.

Then the passage led downwards, at times rather steeply. There were rough steps made in the steepest part so that travellers might not slip too much. But they were so slimy that even a goat

A Journey Under the Sea

would have slipped. Bill came down with a bump, and Philip followed almost immediately.

'Take your foot out of my neck,' said Bill, trying to get up. 'My word, I am in a nice old mess!'

They went on and on. Soon the passage stopped descending, and kept level. It was enclosed in the solid rock. There was no earth, no sand, no chalk – all rock, quite black, and glinting with strange lights now and again.

Once or twice the passage narrowed so much that it was almost impossible to squeeze through. 'Good thing we're not fat,' said Philip, squeezing in his tummy to get by. 'Golly, that was a tight fit! Have the rocks come closer together during the years, Bill – or do you suppose the passage was always narrow there?'

'Always, I should think,' said Bill. 'It's a perfectly natural fissure in the rocky bed under the sea – an amazing one – though I have heard of others like this in different parts of the world. I believe this coast has a good many.'

It was warm in the passage. Here and there the

309

air was not good and the man and the boy began to pant. There seemed to be pockets of airlessness. But on went the two, on and on, their torches gleaming on black, slimy walls, out of which still shone queer phosphorescent lights now and again. Philip began to feel as if he was in a dream. He said so.

'Well, you're not,' came Bill's reassuring voice. 'We're in a peculiar place, but a perfectly real one. It's no dream. Like me to pinch you?'

'Well, I think I would,' said Philip, who really did feel rather odd after so much time in the dark narrow way. So Bill pinched him – and it was a very hard pinch that made Philip yell.

'All right!' he said. 'I'm awake and not dreaming. Nobody would be silly enough to dream *that* pinch.'

Suddenly Bill felt something running by his feet, and he looked down in great astonishment, swinging his torch downwards too. To his enormous surprise he saw a small mouse looking up at him. Bill stopped in astonishment.

'Look here,' he said. 'A mouse. A mouse down *here*! What does it live on? It's a most incredible thing. I simply cannot imagine any animal living down in this passage under the sea.'

Philip chuckled. 'It's all right! It's only Woffly, my pet mouse. It must have run down my sleeve and hopped out.'

'Well, it had better hop in again, if it wants to live,' said Bill. 'No animal could last down here for long.'

'Oh, it will come back when it wants to,' said Philip. 'It won't leave me for long.'

They had to have two or three rests, for the way was tiring and difficult. It went curiously straight for a time and then seemed to go in jerks, having little bits that went off at right angles for a few feet, only to come to the straight again. Philip began to wonder how long his torch would last. He felt suddenly frightened at the thought of being left in the dark down there. Supposing Bill's torch gave out as well?

But Bill reassured him. 'I've got another battery in my pocket,' he told Philip, 'so don't worry. We shall be all right. And that reminds me – I've got a packet of boiled sweets somewhere. I can't help feeling it would make this awful journey easier if we sucked one or two.'

There was a pause whilst Bill searched his pockets. He found the sweets, and soon the two of them were sucking away hard. Certainly it made things easier, somehow, to have a nice big boiled sweet tucked away in his mouth, Philip thought.

'How far do you think we've gone?' asked Philip. 'Halfway?'

'Can't tell,' said Bill. 'Hallo – what's this?'

He paused and shone his torch in front of him. The way appeared to be blocked. 'Gosh! – it looks like a roof-fall,' said Bill. 'Well, if it is, we're done. We've got nothing to clear up the mess with, to see if we can get by.'

But, to their great relief, the fall was very slight, and with the combined strength of both of them, the main rock that stopped their progress was removed to one side, and they managed to clear it.

'I say,' said Philip, after a long time of groping along the passage, 'do you notice that the rocks are changing colour, Bill? They're not black any longer. They're greenish. Do you think that means we are nearing the mines?'

'Yes, I think it probably does,' said Bill. 'It's distinctly hopeful. I don't know how many hours we have been so far – it seems about a hundred at least – but I do think it's about time we were nearing that wretched island.'

'I'm glad we had such a good breakfast,' said Philip. 'I'm beginning to feel very hungry again now, though. I wish we had brought some food with us.'

'I've got plenty of chocolate,' said Bill. 'I'll give you some presently – if it hasn't melted. It's so hot down here now that I shouldn't be surprised if it has.'

It had certainly got very soft, but it hadn't melted. It was good chocolate – slightly bitter, but really delicious to the hungry boy. He went on the dreary way, feeling the slimy walls, noticing the coppery gleams in them, wondering how much longer it would be before the end came.

'Have you by any chance got that map on you?'

called Bill suddenly. 'I forgot to tell you to take it. We shall need it soon.'

'Yes. It's in my pocket,' said Philip. 'Hallo, look – the passage is widening out tremendously!'

It was. It suddenly ended and came out into a big open space, evidently the end of the mine-workings. It must have been here that the copper had run out, thought Philip. What big mines they must have been – and how rich at one time!

'Well – here we are at last,' said Bill, in a low voice. 'And remember that from now on we don't make any noise, Philip. We must find Jack, if we can, without attracting any attention at all.'

Philip felt astonished. 'But, Bill,' he said, 'why can't you just go to the part of the mine where your friends are working and ask them where old Freckles is? Why all the hush-hush, mustn't-talk-loudly business? I don't understand.'

'Well, I have my reasons,' said Bill. 'So please respect them, Philip, even if you don't know what they are. Come on – where's that map?'

Philip pulled it from his pocket. Bill took it,

opened it, spread it on a conveniently flat rock, shone his torch on it and studied it very carefully. At last he put his finger on a certain place.

'Look,' he said. 'That's where we are – see? Right at the end of the workings. I think this bit here shows the beginning of the under-sea passage, but I'm not sure. Now, tell me – which of these many ways did you take when you came into the mines from the shaft-hole?'

'Well – there's the shaft we went down,' said Philip, pointing to where it was marked on the map. 'And here's the main passage we kept to – and there is the cave with the bright light – and it was somewhere about there we heard the clattering, banging noise of men at work.'

'Good,' said Bill, pleased. 'I have quite a clear idea of where to go now. Come along – as quietly as possible. We will make for the main passage, and then see if we can spot Jack anywhere about – or hear of him.'

They made their way very carefully up the wide main passage, off which many side galleries went.

Bill held his finger over the beam of his torch so as not to make too much light. They were not yet near the cave where the children had seen the bright light and heard noises. But they would come to it sooner or later, Philip knew.

'Sh!' suddenly said Bill, stopping so quickly that Philip bumped into him. 'I can hear something. It sounded like footsteps.'

They stood and listened. It was weird standing there in the darkness, hearing the muffled boom of the great waters moving restlessly on the rocky bed of the sea overhead. Philip thought he could hear a noise too – someone's foot kicking against a loose pebble.

Then there was complete silence. So on they went again, and then once more they thought they heard a noise, this time near to them. And Bill felt sure that he could hear someone breathing not far off. He held his own breath to listen.

But perhaps that other, hidden person was holding his breath too, for Bill could hear nothing then. It was very weird. He moved forward silently with Philip.

They came to a sudden corner, and Bill groped round it, for he and Philip had put out their torches as soon as they had heard any noise. And, as Bill reached out to grope for the wall, someone else also reached out, coming in the opposite direction. Then, before Philip knew what was happening, he heard loud exclamations, and felt Bill and somebody else struggling together violently just in front of him. Golly, *now* what was happening?

25

An Extraordinary Find

And now – what had happened to Jack and Kiki all this time? A great deal – some of it most astonishing and unbelievable.

Jack had not known that the others had escaped – in fact, he had not even known that they had been imprisoned. He had wandered off after the parrot, and had become quite lost. The men, as we know, had heard Kiki squealing and shouting some hours later, when they had been chasing Philip and the girls, but they had gone down the wrong passage after them and had not seen them.

So there was poor Jack, lost and terrified, with a forlorn Kiki clutching hard at his shoulder. The boy wandered down a maze of galleries, coming to more and more old abandoned workings. He was afraid that his torch would give out. He was afraid of the roof falling in on top of him.

He was afraid of a great many things.

'I may be lost for ever down here,' he thought. 'I may be wandering miles away from that main passage.'

He suddenly came to a great hole in the roof above him, and realised that he had come to another shaft. 'Of course – there were quite a number of them,' Jack thought, his heart beginning to thump. 'Thank goodness – now I can climb up and get out into the open air.'

But, to the boy's dismay, there was no way of getting up the shaft. Whatever ladder or rope there had once been had rotted or fallen away – there was absolutely no way of climbing up.

It was awful to stand there at the bottom, knowing that freedom, daylight and fresh air were at the top, and yet with no means of reaching them.

'If I were a baby, I bet I'd burst into tears,' said Jack out loud, feeling something suspiciously like tears pricking at the back of his eyelids. 'But I won't do it. I must just grin and bear it.'

He gave a determined grin. Kiki listened to his

words with her head on one side.

'Put the kettle on,' she said sympathetically. That made Jack give a really good grin.

'You *are* an idiot,' he said affectionately. 'Now, the thing is – where do we go next? I feel as if I am probably wandering in the same passage over and over again. But wait a minute – the shafts are all on the island itself – so I must have retraced my steps somehow, because we were all under the sea-bed at one time. As far as I remember, those shafts all connected up with one more or less straight tunnel. I'll go down here – and see if by any chance I come to the main shaft. If I do, I can go up it.'

Jack stumbled on, and came to a blocked-up part, impossible to get by. So he had to go back a good way and start out again, only to come to another roof-fall. It was very disheartening. Kiki became tired of this long journey in the dark passages, and gave a realistic yawn.

'Put your hand before your mouth,' she told herself severely. 'How many times have I told you to shut the door? God save the Queen.'

'Well, your yawn made me yawn too,' said Jack, and he sat down. 'What about a rest, Kiki? I'm getting terribly tired.'

He leaned back against the rocky wall and shut his eyes. He fell into a doze, which lasted an hour or two. When he awoke he hardly knew where he was, and felt frightened when he remembered. He got to his feet, with Kiki still firmly on his shoulder.

'Now, it's no good getting into a panic,' he told himself sternly. 'Just go on walking, and sooner or later you will get somewhere.'

It was whilst he was stumbling through the many passages that Kiki heard the noise of the men chasing the children, and shouted loudly. But Jack heard nothing, and turned off into a winding passage just before the men came up. He did not know that he was near to the wide shaft-hole – but presently he came to the big main passage, and stopped.

'Can this be the wide passage we saw on the map?' he thought. 'It may be. If only I had a brighter torch! I hope to goodness it's not going to fade out. It doesn't seem so bright as it was.'

He went down the passage, and saw some rough-hewn steps in the rock, leading upwards. Out of curiosity the boy climbed them, and came to another passage, which evidently led to yet another working. He stumbled and fell against the wall, dislodging a stone or small rock, which fell down with a crash. Jack held up his torch to see where it had fallen from, afraid that the roof was caving in.

But it wasn't. His torch gleamed on to something that shone coppery-red – a large, irregular kind of stone, thought Jack. And then he suddenly realised that it wasn't a stone – it was – yes, it must be – a large copper nugget! Golly, what a beauty! Could he possibly carry it?

With trembling hands the boy prised the nugget carefully away from its place. It was on a kind of shelf made by a crack in the rock just there. Had someone hidden it there, years ago? Or had it been placed there by one of the men working the mines now? Or was it there naturally, a real nugget in the depths of the earth? Jack didn't know.

It was heavy, but he could carry it. A nugget

of copper! The boy kept repeating the words to himself. Almost as good as finding a Great Auk – not quite as thrilling of course, but almost. What would the others say?

Jack thought he had better keep out of the way of the miners more than ever now. They might take the nugget from him. It might legally be theirs, of course, but he did want to have the thrill of showing it to the others as his find before he gave it up to anyone.

The boy went back to the main passage with the nugget in his hands. He had to put his torch into his belt now, as he could not carry it as well as the copper, and it was difficult to make his way along, because the torch shone almost directly downwards instead of forwards.

'Hallo!' said Jack, stopping suddenly as he heard a noise in the distance. 'I rather think I'm coming towards that clattering noise we heard before – where the men are working. Perhaps I'm near the other children too.'

The boy crept forward. He went into a passage

that turned suddenly round a corner – and there before him was the brilliantly lighted cave again. Last time he had seen it, it had been empty – this time there were men there. They were undoing the boxes and crates that the children had seen there before. Jack watched, wondering what was in them.

'I'm in the same passage as I was when Kiki flew off and I went after her,' thought Jack. 'I do wonder what has happened to the others. Golly, but it's good to see a bright light again. If I crouch here, behind this jutting rock, I don't believe anyone will see me.'

Kiki was absolutely quiet. The brilliant light frightened her after being so long in the darkness. She crouched on the boy's shoulder, watching.

There were tins in the boxes and crates – tins of meat and fruit. Jack felt very hungry when he saw them, for he had had nothing to eat for a long time. The men opened a few of the tins, poured the contents out on to tin plates, and began to eat, talking to each other. Jack could not hear what they were saying. He felt so hungry that he almost walked

out to the men to beg for some of their food.

But they didn't look very nice men. They wore trousers only, belted at the waist, and nothing else. It was so hot in the mines that it was impossible to wear many clothes. Jack wished he could wear only shorts, but he knew he would not like Kiki's claws on his bare shoulder.

The men finished their meal, and then went down a passage or gallery at the further end of the cave they were in. There was no one there now. The clattering, banging noise began again. Evidently the men were at work once more.

Jack crept into the brilliantly lighted cave. The light came from these three lamps hung from the roof. Jack looked into the opened tins. There was a little meat left in one and some pineapple chunks in another. He finished them up quickly. He thought that never in his life had he tasted anything so delicious as the food in those tins.

He decided to creep over to the passage down which the men had gone back to work. It would be exciting to see how men worked in a copper mine. Did they use pickaxes? Did they blast out the copper? What were they doing to make all that noise? It really sounded as if it came from some big machine busily at work.

He crept down the passage, and then found that he was looking into another cave. He was most astonished at what he saw. There were about a dozen men there, busy with a number of machines that clattered and banged, making quite a deafening noise that echoed round the cave.

There was an engine of some sort which added to the din. 'What strange machinery!' thought Jack, staring. 'How ever in the world did they get it all down here into the mines? They must have brought it down in pieces, and then put them together here. Golly, how busy it all is, and what a noise it makes!'

Jack watched in wonder. Were they extracting copper by means of this machine? He knew vaguely that many metals had to be roasted or smelted or worked in some way before they were pure. He supposed they were doing that. It was plain, then, that the copper in these mines was not usually found in big nuggets, such as the one Jack was even now holding.

One of the men wiped his forehead and came from the machine towards Jack's hiding-place. The boy darted away, and went into a small blind passage to wait till the man had passed. He came back carrying a mug of water. Jack waited in the little blind passage for a minute or two, leaning against what he thought was the wall. But suddenly the 'wall' gave way a little, and the boy slipped backwards. Then, putting his torch on, he found that it was no wall but a strong wooden door, leading into a cell-like place – rather like the one in which the other children had been imprisoned.

Hearing footsteps, he hurriedly went into the cell and pushed the door shut. The footsteps went by. Jack switched on his torch again to see what was in the cave.

It was stacked with bundles upon bundles of crisp papers, the same size put together and the same colours, tightly fastened together. Jack looked

at them – and then he looked again, blinking his eyes in amazement.

In that cell-like cave were thousands of bundles of paper money. There were bundles of five-pound notes, bundles of ten-pound notes – there they were, neatly stacked together, a fortune great enough to make anyone a millionaire in a night.

'Now I really must be dreaming,' thought Jack, rubbing his eyes. 'There's no doubt about it. I'm in a very extraordinary dream. In a minute I shall wake up and laugh. People simply don't find things like this – treasure in a cave underground. Why, I might be in the middle of some wonderful fairy story. It's quite impossible – I'd better wake up immediately.'

26

A Bad Time – and
a Surprising Meeting

But Jack didn't wake up – and for a very good reason too. He wasn't asleep.

He was wide awake and staring at this colossal fortune in paper money. It didn't make sense. Why was it all stored here, in this cave underground? Who did it belong to? Why didn't they put it into a bank in the usual way?

'Perhaps the men working this mine are finding a lot of copper and selling it secretly, and keeping the money here that they get for it,' thought Jack. He was so lost in amazement at the sight of such a fortune piled up there in front of him that he did not hear someone coming to the door of the cave he was in.

The man who opened the door and saw Jack in the cave was even more surprised than Jack himself. He stood staring at the boy with his mouth wide open, and his eyes almost falling out of his head. Then he dragged the boy roughly out of the cell, and pulled him to the room where the machine was working.

'Look here!' yelled the man. 'Look here! I found him in the store room.'

The machine was stopped at once. The men gathered round Jack and his captor. One of them stepped forward. It was Jake.

He looked very evil and the black patch he wore over one eye made him look most peculiar. He shook Jack so roughly that the boy lost his breath completely and sank down on the ground when Jake let go of his arm.

'Where are the rest of you?' said Jake. 'You tell me, see! Who are you with? What are you doing down here? What do you know?'

Jack picked up his nugget, looked round for Kiki, who had flown in fright to the roof of the cave, and tried to think what to answer for the best. The men took no notice of his big copper nugget, which surprised Jack very much. He had been afraid they would take it away from him at once.

'I don't know where the others are,' he said at last. 'We came to the island together, two boys and two girls, and I got separated from the others.'

'Who else was with you?' demanded Jake. 'You kids didn't come here by yourselves.'

'We did,' insisted Jack. 'I say – who does all that money in there belong to?'

The listening men made some low, threatening noises, and Jack gazed round uneasily. Jake's face grew black. He looked round at the men.

'Something's up,' he said, and the men nodded. He turned again to Jack. 'Now look here,' he said, 'you know a lot more than you've told us – you've picked up something from the others, haven't you? – well, you just tell us all you know, or you may never see daylight again. See? Is that clear?'

It was horribly clear. Jack began to tremble. Kiki gave a screech that made everyone jump.

'I don't know what you mean,' said Jack desperately. 'All we knew was that someone was working these copper mines again, getting copper, and that Bill Smugs was taking food here in his boat. That's honestly all I know.'

'Bill Smugs,' repeated Jake. 'That's what the other kids said. Who *is* this Bill Smugs?'

Jack was puzzled. 'Isn't that his real name?' he said.

'What's his real name?' suddenly said Jake, so threateningly that Jack dropped his precious nugget in a panic, thinking the man was going to strike him. It fell on the edge of Jake's foot and the man picked it up and had a look at it.

'What's this stone you're carrying about?' he said, in curiosity. 'Are you kids mad? A parrot – and a heavy stone – Bill Smugs – copper mines. You're all crazy.'

'I think this kid knows more than he's said,' said Olly, stepping beside Jake. 'What about locking him up without any food for a day or so? That will make him talk. Or what about a good beating?'

Jack went pale, but he did not show that he was afraid. 'I don't know any more than I've already told you,' he said. 'What *is* there to know, anyway? What's the mystery?'

'Take him away,' said Jake roughly. 'He'll talk when he's half-starved.'

Olly took the boy by the shoulder and led him roughly from the cave, prodding him unkindly as he did so. He led him to the same cell-like cave in which the other children had been imprisoned. Just as he was pushing the boy in, Kiki flew down and hacked viciously at the man's face with her curved beak. Olly put up his hands to protect himself, and dropped his torch. It went out.

Jack slipped swiftly to the side and crouched outside the cell in silence. Kiki did not know where

he was. She flew into the cell and perched on the table there, in complete darkness.

'Now then, now then, what a pity!' she said loudly. The cell door banged. Olly had shut it on the parrot, thinking that it was Jack talking inside there. He had not even known that the bird could talk.

He turned the key in the lock. Kiki was still talking away softly, though neither Jack nor Olly could hear the words. As Olly was turning away, Jake came up.

'Did you put him in?' he asked, and flashed his torch on to the shut door.

'Yes,' said Olly. 'He's gassing away to himself in there – you can hear him – I think he's mad.'

The men listened, and Kiki's voice came clearly from the cell. 'What a pity, what a pity!'

'He's sorry for himself, isn't he?' said Jake, and then he gave such a horrible laugh that Jack's heart went cold with fear. 'He'll be sorrier still soon.'

The men went back to the machine cave and soon the clattering, banging noises began again.

Jack stood up. Kiki had saved him from a horrible punishment – poor Kiki. She didn't know she had saved him. Jack moved to the door, meaning to unlock it and get the parrot out.

But the key was gone. One of the men must have taken it. So Kiki was a prisoner, a real prisoner, and would have to stay there till someone let her out.

But anyway Jack himself was free. 'There's something wrong about all this business,' the boy thought. 'Something wrong about all that money – and those mysterious machines. The men are bad. They can't be friends of Bill's. We've made a mistake.'

He went down the passage carefully, not daring to switch on his torch. If only he could find the shaft-hole and go up it. Perhaps the others would be at the top, waiting for him? Or had they gone back home and left him all alone? Was it still daytime or was it night?

Jack stumbled along passage after passage, wishing that Kiki was with him for company. He felt lonely and afraid now. He wanted to talk to somebody. He wanted to see the others.

At last he was so tired that he could not go on. He curled up in a corner of a small cave, shut his eyes and fell into a restless, uncomfortable kind of sleep. For hours he slept, tired out, his limbs getting stiff as he lay there. And Kiki slept too, in the cave, puzzled and angry, missing her master as much as he missed her.

When Jack awoke he put up his hand to feel Kiki, as he often did – but the bird was not on his shoulder. Then he remembered. Kiki was a prisoner. Because of her and her ability to talk like a human being, he, Jack was free.

He knew a lot. He knew about the hidden treasure. He knew about those machines which were so well hidden in these underground caves for some sinister reason. He knew that the men working them were bad men. If they thought their secret, whatever it was, had been discovered, they would not stop at anything.

'The thing I've got to do, the thing I really must do, is to escape and tell what I know,' thought Jack.

'I somehow think I ought to go to the police. I'd like to go and tell Bill – because I think now he's not in league with those men – but I'm still not certain. Anyway, the thing is – I've got to tell *some*body.'

So once more the boy began his endless wandering in the workings of the mines. Up and down long, musty passages he went, his torch now giving him only a very poor light.

And then suddenly it gave out altogether. Jack tapped it a little. He screwed and unscrewed the bottom. But the battery was dead – no light would come from his torch unless he put in a new battery – and certainly he could not do that at the moment.

Jack really did feel afraid then. There was only one hope now of escape, and that was to find, by good luck, the shaft leading up to the open air. But that was a very poor chance indeed.

He wandered on, groping his way, his hand out before his face, carrying the nugget uncomfortably under his arm, holding it there with his other hand. Then he thought he heard something. He stopped and listened. No – it was nothing.

He went on again, and suddenly stopped. He couldn't help feeling that people were near. Was that somebody breathing? He stood in the dark, holding his breath and listening. But he heard nothing. 'Maybe,' he thought, 'the other person is holding his breath and listening too.'

He went on – and suddenly he bumped hard into somebody. Was it Jake, or Olly? He began to struggle desperately and the other person held on to him firmly, hurting his arm. The nugget dropped to the ground and hit Jack's foot.

'Oh, my foot, my foot!' groaned poor Jack.

There was an astonished silence. Then a powerful torch was switched on by his captor, and a voice said in amazement, 'Why, it's Jack!'

'Freckles!' came Philip's voice too, and he ran to Jack and gave him an affectionate slap on the back. 'Freckles! What luck to come across you like this!'

'Tufty! And Bill!' said Jack, his voice breaking in a great gasp of joy and relief. Oh, the delight of hearing a familiar voice after so many hours of lonely darkness! The joy of seeing Philip, his tuft of hair sticking up from his forehead as usual! And Bill, with his familiar grin, his twinkling eyes, and his good dependable feeling of grown-upness – Jack was glad to have a grown-up to help him. Children could meddle in things to a certain extent – but there often came a time when you had to lean on the grown-ups.

He gave a gulp, and Bill patted him on the back. 'Fine to see you, Jack. I bet you've got plenty to tell us.'

'I have,' said Jack. He took out his handkerchief and blew his nose hard. Then he felt better. 'Where are the girls?'

'Safe at home,' said Philip. 'We missed you somehow down in the mines yesterday, Jack, and we got taken prisoner, but we escaped, got up the shaft-hole, found our boat and sailed away in the half-dark. I went to find old Bill, and here he is. We couldn't come in his boat because it was smashed by someone – and Joe's boat was gone too.'

'Well – how did you come then?' asked Jack in astonishment.

'There's a way under the sea from Craggy-Tops to here,' said Philip. 'What do you think of that? We found it in an old book about Craggy-Tops. It took us ages to come. It was very weird. I didn't like it much. But here we are.'

Jack was really amazed to hear how they had come. He questioned them eagerly. But Bill had a few questions to ask Jack. 'This is all much more important than you think, Jack,' he said. 'Let's sit down. I've got an idea you can solve a big mystery for me.'

27

A Lot of Things Are Made Clear

'I've got some weird things to tell you,' said Jack eagerly. 'First of all, what do you think I found? A cave absolutely chock full of money – paper money – notes, you know. Well, I should think there must have been thousands and thousands of pounds' worth there – you've simply no idea.'

'Ah,' said Bill Smugs, in a voice full of satisfaction. 'Ah! Now that really *is* news. Fine, Jack!'

'Then I saw a lot of machines at work,' went on Jack, pleased to find that his news was so intensely interesting to Bill. 'And an engine. I thought it was to smelt or roast the copper, or whatever they have to do with it, but one of the machines looked like a printing-press.'

'Ah-*ha*! said Bill, with even greater satisfaction in his voice. 'This is wonderful news. Amazing! Jack, you've solved a five-year-old mystery – a mystery that has been puzzling the Government and the whole of the police for a long time.'

'What mystery?' asked Jack.

'I bet I know,' put in Philip excitedly. 'Bill, that machinery is for printing false paper money, isn't it? – counterfeit notes – dud money. And the money, in notes, that Jack found, is stored there after being printed. It will be taken from this island and used by the crooks or their masters.'

'You've just about hit it,' said Bill. 'We've been after this gang for years – couldn't find where they had their printing-outfit installed – couldn't make out where the money appeared from. It's excellently done – only an expert can tell the difference between a real bank-note and these dud ones.'

'Bill! So the men aren't working the copper mines, then!' cried Jack, in astonishment. 'We were wrong about that. They chose these old mines, not to work any copper in them, but to hide their printing machines, and to do all their work in safety. How clever! How awfully clever!'

'Very smart indeed,' said Bill grimly. 'All they

needed was a go-between – someone who could sail out to the island with food for them, and other necessities – and take away back to the Boss, whoever he is, stacks of the dud notes. Well – it was the go-between that gave the show away, really.'

'Who's the go-between?' asked Jack interestedly. 'Anyone we know?'

'Of course,' said Bill. 'I should have thought you would have guessed at once – Joe.'

'*Joe!*' cried the two boys, and in a flash they saw how everything fitted in, where Joe was concerned.

'Yes – he had a boat, and he had only to say he was going fishing in it, in order to get over to the island and back,' said Philip. 'He could go at night too, if he wanted to. Those signals Jack saw were from the men on the island – and it was Joe up on the cliff, signalling back, that night Jack met him there.'

'Yes, it was,' said Jack, remembering. 'And when he went off shopping in the car he'd take some of that counterfeit money with him, I guess, and deliver it to his bosses, whoever they were. No wonder he would never take us out in the car with him, or in the boat. He was afraid we might suspect something.'

'Do you remember those boxes and crates down in the second cellar, behind that door he kept hidden by piled-up boxes?' said Philip. 'Well, I bet those didn't belong to Aunt Polly. I bet they were Joe's stores, waiting to be taken across to the island next time he went in his boat.'

'His tales about "things" wandering on the cliffs at nights were only stories to frighten us and keep us from going out at night, and finding out anything he was doing,' went on Jack. 'Gracious, how everything fits in now, doesn't it?'

'It certainly seems to,' said Bill, in an amused voice. He had been listening to this conversation with great interest.

'Why did *you* come to this coast, to live in that tumbledown shack?' asked Jack suddenly. 'Were you really a bird-watcher?'

'Of course not,' said Bill, laughing. 'I didn't bargain on meeting a real bird-lover when I told you I was a bird-watcher. You nearly tripped me up lots of times. I had to read up a whole lot about birds I wasn't in the least interested in, so that you wouldn't suspect I didn't know much about them, Jack. It was really very awkward for me. I couldn't tell you what I really was, of course – a member of the police force, detailed to keep an eye on Joe and see what he was up to.'

'How did you know Joe was up to anything?' asked Philip.

'Well, he's pretty well known to the police,' said Bill. 'He has been mixed up in the counterfeiting of bank-notes before, and we wondered if he had anything to do with this big-scale printing that was going on somewhere, we didn't know where. We thought it just as well to watch him, once we knew where he was. He has a mighty fine way of disappearing. He's been with your aunt for five years now, as odd-job man, and nobody ever suspected he was a fellow with a very bad record. But one of our men spotted him in town one day and found out where he worked. Then down I came, this summer, to keep a quiet eye on him.'

'What a hornet's nest you've stirred up!' said Jack. 'Bill – did we help at all?'

'A lot,' said Bill, 'though you didn't know it. You made me certain that Joe was the go-between. You made me sure that it was the Isle of Gloom he kept going to. So I went there myself one day, and explored the mines a little way. That was when I dropped my pencil, I expect. But I must say I didn't find anything that made me suspect there were men in the mines, doing their illegal bank-note printing on hidden machines.'

'But *we* found out about it,' said Jack proudly. 'What are you going to do about it, Bill?'

'Well,' said Bill, 'last night I spoke over the radio to my chiefs. I told them I was pretty certain what was going on here, and that I was going over to the island to rescue someone from the mines, and would they get busy, please, and begin to clear the matter up?'

'What will they do?' asked Jack, thrilled.

'I shan't know till I get back and report,' said Bill.

'We'd better go now, I think. We'll go back through the sea passage, the way Philip and I came.'

'I suppose it was Joe who smashed your boat up,' said Philip. 'He must have suspected something. I think he knew you were our friend.'

'Joe is a remarkably clever rascal,' said Bill, getting up and stretching himself. 'All the cleverer because he pretends to be stupid. Come along.'

'Bill – I want to get Kiki,' said Jack suddenly. 'I can't leave her here. The men will kill her – or she'll die of starvation or fright. Can't we go and get her?'

'No,' said Bill. 'There are more important things to be done.'

'Let's get her, Bill,' said Philip, who knew that Kiki was to Jack what a dog was to other people. 'We've only got to get out the map, find that main passage, and then slip along to the caves there. Jack will know where the cell is where Kiki got locked in. I think it sounds like the same one the girls and I were imprisoned in.'

'Well – we'd better be quick, then,' said Bill

doubtfully. 'And mind – no noise at all. We don't want to attract attention.'

They spread out the map, traced out where they were, and where the main passage was, and set out. It was not long before they were walking down the wide passage, silently and carefully.

Bill heard the clattering and banging noise. The machines were at work again. He looked grim and listened intently. Yes – that was a printing-press all right.

Just as they were coming to the cell cave in which Kiki was imprisoned, they heard sounds of voices. They crouched against the wall, hardly daring to breathe.

'That's Jake,' whispered Philip, his mouth close against Bill's ear.

There were three men, and they were at the door of the cell where the parrot was. They were listening in astonishment. A voice came from the cell, raised high, and the words could be heard.

'Don't sniff, I tell you! Where's your handkerchief?

How many times have I told you to wipe your feet? Poor old Kiki, poor, poor old Kiki! Put the kettle on!'

'The boy's gone mad,' said Jake, to the other two men. Evidently they still thought they had shut Jack up in the cave.

'Pop goes the weasel!' announced Kiki dramatically, and then made a noise like a runaway engine going through a tunnel and whistling.

'He's off his head,' said Olly, amazed.

There came a terrific screech, and the third man spoke suddenly.

'That's a parrot. That's what it is. The boy has got his parrot in there.'

'Open the door and we'll see,' said Olly. Jake put the key into the lock. The door swung inwards. Kiki at once flew out with a screech that made everyone jump. The men flashed their lamp into the cave.

It was empty. Jake turned fiercely on Olly. 'You fool! You put the parrot in there and let the boy escape. You deserve to be shot.'

Olly stared into the empty cave. It was true. Only the parrot had been there. 'Well,' said Olly. 'I expect the kid is lost for ever in these mines now, and will never be heard of again. Serves him right.'

'We're fools, Olly,' said Jake bitterly. 'First we let those other children trick us, and then the boy.'

They left the door open and went off towards the lighted cave. Jack gave a gasp. Kiki had suddenly flown on to his shoulder, and was making the most affectionate noises. She pretended to bite his ear, she made clicking noises meant to represent kisses, and altogether behaved in a most excited and delighted way. Jack scratched her head, and felt just as delighted himself.

'Now, come along, for heaven's sake,' said Bill, in a low voice. They left the passage and walked quickly away, their torches shining. They had not gone very far before they distinctly heard someone else coming.

'It's somebody from the main shaft, I should think,' said Jack, in a low voice. They put out their torches and waited. The person came nearer,

heavy-footed. His torch shone brightly. They could not see what he was like at all. They tried to slip back into a little blind passage, but Jack stumbled and fell, making a noise. Kiki screeched.

A torch dazzled them, and a voice came sharply out of the darkness. 'Stand where you are or I'll shoot!'

Bill put out a hand to make the boys stand still. There was something in that voice that had to be obeyed. The owner of it would not hesitate to shoot.

The three of them stood blinking there in the passage. Jack recognised the voice, and so did Philip. Who was it?

And then, in a flash, they knew. Of course they knew.

'It's Joe!' cried Jack. 'Joe, what are you doing here?'

'A question I'm going to ask *you*, all three of you,' said Joe, in a cold, grim voice. The light from his torch rested full on Bill's face. 'So *you're* here too,' said Joe. 'I smashed your boat – but I reckon you found the old way under the sea-bed, didn't you? You think yourself mighty clever, all of you – but you've been just a bit *too* clever. There's a nasty time ahead of you – a – very – nasty – time.'

28

Trapped

The light gleamed on a revolver held by Joe. Bill felt angry with himself. If he hadn't agreed to go back for that wretched parrot, this would never have

happened. Joe was tough. He was not likely to be fooled as easily as Jake had been.

'Turn round, hold your hands above your heads and walk in front of me,' ordered Joe. 'Ah – there's that parrot. I owe it quite a lot – well, I'll pay me debt now.'

Jack knew Joe meant to shoot Kiki and he gave the parrot a blow that surprised her very much. Kiki rose high into the air in indignation, screeching, lost in the darkness. 'Keep away, Kiki, keep away!' yelled Jack.

Kiki remained lost in the darkness. Something warned her that Jack did not want her near him. She sensed danger. She followed the little company, keeping well behind Joe, flying from place to place as silent as a bat.

The three of them were soon shut in the now familiar cave. Joe, who had shouted for Jake, locked the door himself. Then the prisoners heard them going off.

'Well, we're in a pretty pickle now, I'm afraid,' said Bill. 'Why in the world did I agree to go back for that parrot? We may all lose our lives because of that, and these fellows may escape scot-free with their thousands of false bank-notes, to spread them all over the country. We really are up against it now.'

'I'm sorry I asked you to go back for Kiki,' said Jack humbly.

'I'm as much to blame as you,' said Bill, lighting a cigarette. 'Golly, it's hot down here.'

After what seemed to be an endless time, the door was opened again, and Joe came in, with Jake, Olly and two or three more men behind him.

'We just want to say a fond goodbye to you,' said Joe, his face gleaming in the lamp-light. 'We've finished up our business here. You came in at the end, Bill Smugs the cop, too late to do anything. We've got all the notes we'll ever be able to use now.'

'So you're clearing out, are you?' said Bill quietly. 'Smashing up the machines to hide your tracks – taking away all your stores and your packets of dud notes. You won't escape so easily. Your machines will be found all right, smashed or not, and your ...'

'Nothing will ever be found, Bill Smugs,' said Joe. 'Not a thing. The whole of the police force can come to this island, but they'll never find anything they can trace back to us – never!'

'Why?' asked Bill, unable to conceal his surprise.

'Because we're flooding the mines,' said Joe, smiling wickedly and showing his teeth. 'Yes, Bill Smugs, these mines will soon be flooded – water will pour into every tunnel, every passage, every cave. It will hide our machines, and all traces of our work. I am afraid it will hide you too.'

'You're not going to leave us here, surely,' said Bill. 'Leave me, if you like – but take the boys up with you.'

'We don't want any of you,' said Joe, still in the same horribly polite tones. 'You would be in the way.'

'You couldn't be as cruel as that!' cried Bill. 'Why, they're only children.'

'I have my orders,' said Joe. He did not seem at all the same stupid, grumpy fellow that the boys knew before – he was a different Joe altogether, and not at all a pleasant one.

'How do you propose to flood the mines?' asked Bill.

'Easily,' replied Joe. 'We have mined part of the passage through which you came from Craggy-Tops, under the sea-bed. When we are safely above ground, you will hear the muffled roar of a great explosion. The dynamite will blow a hole in the roof of that under-sea passage – and the sea will pour through. As you will guess, it will rush into these mines, and fill them up to sea level. I am afraid you will not find things very pleasant then.'

Jack tried to stand up to show Joe that he was not afraid, but his knees wouldn't hold him. He was afraid, very much afraid. And so was Philip. Only Bill kept a really brave front. He laughed.

'Well – do your worst. You won't escape so easily as you think. More is known about you and this gang and its bosses than you imagine.'

One of the men said something to Joe. He nodded. The boys felt certain that the time was soon coming when the sea-bed was due to be blasted open –

and then the waters would roar down and find their way into every nook and cranny.

'Well – goodbye,' said Joe, grinning and showing his teeth again.

'See you soon,' replied Bill, in just as polite a tone. The boys did not say anything. Kiki, out in the passage, gave a cackling laugh.

'I should have liked to kill that bird before I left,' muttered Joe, and went out of the cave with the others. He slammed the door and locked it.

There was the sound of retreating footsteps and then silence. Bill looked at the boys.

'Cheer up,' he said. 'We're not dead yet. We'll give those fellows time to get some distance away, and then I'll open this door and out we'll go.'

'Open the door? How?' asked Jack.

'Oh, I've my little way,' grinned Bill, and pulled out a queer collection of files and spindly keys. After a minute or two he set to work on the door, and in a very short time it was swinging open.

'Now for the shaft,' said Bill. 'Come on, before it's too late.'

They made their way to the main passage and then half walked, half ran towards the big shaft. It took some time to get there.

Just as they reached it, and looked upwards to where the faintest gleam of daylight showed, there came a curious sound.

It was a muffled roar, deep, deep down in the mines. It echoed round and about in a frightening way.

'Well – Joe spoke the truth,' said Bill soberly. 'That was the dynamite going off. If it really has blown a hole in the sea-bed, the waters will even now be rushing up that under-sea passage to the mines.'

'Come on, then,' said Philip, eager to get up into the open air. 'Come on. I want to get into the sunshine.'

'I must tie my nugget round me somewhere,' said Jack, who was still manfully carrying the heavy piece of copper. 'Why – what's the matter, Bill?'

Bill had given a sharp exclamation that startled the boys. 'Look there,' said Bill, shining his torch on to the first few feet of the shaft-hole. 'Those men have gone up the shaft – and have carefully hacked away the ladder near the bottom so that we couldn't climb up, even if we did escape from the cave. They were leaving nothing to chance. We're done. We can't escape. There's no way of climbing up without a ladder.'

In despair the three of them gazed at the smashed-up rungs. Kiki gave a mournful screech that made them jump.

'Bill – I believe we might find some kind of a ladder in that big open cave where the boxes and crates of food were,' said Jack desperately. 'I believe I saw one. Shall we go back and see? I don't expect the men have done more than smash up the beginning rungs of the shaft-hole ladder – they'd know we couldn't use the ladder higher up if there was nothing to climb on lower down.'

'Are you sure there was a ladder in that cave?' asked Philip. 'I don't remember one.'

'Well – it's our only chance,' said Bill. 'Come on – back we go to find it.'

But they didn't reach the cave. They only went down the main passage a little way and then they stopped in horror. Something was swirling towards them – something black and strange and powerful.

'The waters are in already,' yelled Bill. 'Come back. Get to the highest part. My word, the whole sea is emptying itself into the mines.'

The gurgling sound of water trickling down all the passages and into every cave was now plainly to be heard. It was a greedy, sucking sound, a sound that frightened even Bill. The three of them ran back to the main shaft at once. It was higher than the rest of the ground round about – but soon the water would reach there too.

'It will find its own level, anyway,' said Bill. 'All these shafts go down below sea level, a long way below – and the mines will certainly fill up to the level of the sea. I reckon it will half-fill these shaft-holes too.'

'But Bill – we shall all be drowned!' said Jack, in a trembling voice.

'Can you swim?' asked Bill. 'Yes – of course you

both can. Well, listen, there's just one hope for us. When the water fills up this shaft, we must rise with it – let it take us up. We can keep afloat all right, I think, if we don't get panicky. Then, when we reach the part of the ladder undamaged by the men, we can climb up. Now, do you think you can keep your heads, and, when the water comes, go up the shaft-hole with it?'

'Yes,' said the boys pluckily. Jack turned and looked nervously down the passage. He could see the black water in the distance, gleaming in the light of Bill's torch. It looked very horrible, somehow.

'That's the end of these mines, then, Bill, isn't it?' said Philip. 'No one will ever be able to come down here again.'

'Well, they were worked out anyway,' said Bill. 'Jack was lucky to find a nugget to take back to show everyone. It was probably hidden by a long-ago miner who forgot where he had hidden it – and years and years afterwards Jack found it.'

'I *must* take it back with me,' said Jack. 'I simply

must. But I know I can't hold it and swim too. It's too heavy.'

Bill stripped off his jersey and his vest. He wrapped the nugget in his vest, knotted it, then tied a thick piece of string round it. He put his jersey on again and then hung the nugget round his neck.

'Bit heavy,' said he, with a grin, 'but quite safe. You carry Kiki, I'll carry the nugget.'

'Thanks awfully,' said Jack. 'Sure it won't drag you down under the water?'

'I hardly think so,' said Bill, who was immensely strong.

'The water's coming nearer,' said Philip uneasily. 'Look!'

They all looked. It was advancing near to the little bit of rising ground under the shaft where they stood.

'Isn't it awfully black?' said Jack. 'I suppose it's the darkness that makes it look so black. It looks simply horrid.'

'It will take a bit of time to get to our shaft,'

said Bill. 'Let's sit down and rest a bit whilst we've a chance.'

They sat down. Philip's mouse ran out of his sleeve, and then sat up on its hind legs, sniffing. Kiki saw it and gave a squeal.

'Wipe your feet, I tell you!' she said.

'Now, don't you frighten Woffly,' said Philip. The three of them watched the antics of the mouse whilst they waited. The water lapped nearer, sucking and gurgling in the passages.

'It must be absolutely *pouring* down the hole in the roof of the under-sea passage,' said Philip. 'I say, Bill – will the water rush the other way too – down the under-sea passage to Craggy-Tops – and make the well salt water?'

'Well, yes – I suppose it will,' said Bill, considering. 'The well is below sea level, of course – so the sea is bound to pour into it, through the entrance in the well-shaft. That's bad, Philip. It will mean that you and your people won't have well water any more – I can't think what you'll do.'

'Here comes the water to our feet now,' said

Jack, watching a wave sweep up to them. 'Kiki, do sit still on my shoulder. Tufty, where's Woffly?'

'Down my neck now,' said Philip. 'Ooh, isn't the water cold!'

The mines were hot, so the water did feel cold – icy-cold. Philip, Jack and Bill stood up and watched it swirling round their ankles. It rose gradually to their knees. It rose above them.

The three were standing right under the shaft, waiting for the moment to come when the water would lift them up, enabling them to swim, or tread water.

'I'm frozen,' said Philip. 'I never knew such cold water.'

'It isn't really cold,' said Bill, 'but we feel so hot down here that the water strikes us as very cold. It hasn't had time to warm up yet.'

The water rose to their waists and then more rapidly to their shoulders.

'God save the Queen!' said Kiki, in a horrified tone, looking down from Jack's shoulder at the restless black water below her.

Soon Bill and the boys were lifted off their feet, and swam with difficulty on the surface of the water in the shaft. 'There's so little room,' panted Jack. 'We're all on top of one another.'

They were certainly very crowded and it was tiring work trying to keep afloat when there was really no room for swimming. The water rose steadily. Bill had taken Philip's little torch and placed it between his teeth, so that its light shone round on the shaft-wall. He wanted to see whether the ladder was still smashed, far up the shaft, or whether the men had only damaged the lower part.

He took the torch from his mouth at last. 'We're all right,' he said. 'The ladder's not smashed here. We have risen some way up the shaft with the water, and now we can get on to the ladder. I'll help you each up. Go first, Jack, with Kiki. She's getting so scared.'

Jack splashed his way to the side of the shaft where the ladder was. Bill shone the torch there. Jack clung to the rungs and began to haul himself up. Then, when he had climbed a good way up, Philip followed. Last of all Bill hauled himself up, feeling the drag of the heavy copper nugget on his neck. It had been extremely difficult to keep afloat with it, but somehow he had managed.

Up they went – and up and up. It seemed ages before they were anywhere near the top. They soon stopped shivering, and got hot with climbing. Their wet clothes stuck to them uncomfortably. Kiki talked in Jack's ear, very sorry for herself. She did not like this part of the adventure at all.

Philip's mouse didn't like it either. It had clung to Philip's ear during his stay in the water, when the boy's head had been the only thing above the surface – and now it didn't at all approve of such wet clothes. It couldn't seem to find a nice, dry, warm place anywhere.

'We're almost there,' Jack shouted down at last. 'Not far now.'

That was cheerful news. They hurried on, feeling new strength in their arms and legs now that they knew their long and tiring climb was nearing an end.

Jack climbed out first, Kiki flying off his shoulder with a glad squeal. Then he stopped in astonishment. A man was sitting quietly by the head of the shaft, a revolver in his hand.

'Hands up!' said the man, in a stern voice. 'Don't dare to warn anyone following you. Stand there. Hands up, I said!'

29

All's Well That Ends Well

Jack stood with his hands above his head, his mouth open in horror. Had they escaped only to get caught again? He did not dare to shout.

Philip climbed out and was treated in the same way; he too was shocked and dismayed. The man with the revolver waited in silence, covering the boys with his weapon, watching to see who would come out next. Bill climbed out, his back to the man. He received the same order.

'Hands up! Don't dare to warn anyone following. Stand there!'

Bill swung round. He had put his hands up at once, but now he put them down and grinned.

'It's all right, Sam,' he said. 'Put up your gun.'

Sam gave an exclamation, and put his revolver into his belt. He held out his hand to Bill.

'It's *you*!' he said. 'I was left here in case any more

fellows of the gang came up. I didn't expect *you* to bob up.'

The boys stared, open-mouthed. What was all this?

'Did you get a shock?' said Bill, noticing their surprise. 'This is Sam – one of our detectives – great friend of mine. Well, Sam – seeing you here gives me great hopes. What's happened?'

'Come and see,' said Sam, with a grin, and he led the way. They all went through the pass in the hills, following the burly Sam. They came out on to open ground, and made their way towards the coast.

They came suddenly on a truly interesting sight. Lined up in a row, their faces sullen, were all the men from the mines. Joe was there too, fierce anger in his face. Two men stood nearby, each with a revolver. All weapons had been taken from the prisoners.

'There's Joe!' cried Philip. Joe looked at him with a scowl that turned to surprise. So the boys and their friend had escaped! Joe was immensely surprised and racked his brains to think how anyone could have got out of a locked cave in a flooded mine and up a shaft whose ladder was completely smashed at the bottom.

'How were they caught?' asked Jack, in wonder. Kiki saw Joe and flew round his head, screeching and hooting and yelling. She recognised her old enemy, and knew he could no longer harm her.

Sam grinned at Jack's wonder. 'Well, Bill Cunningham here,' he said with a nod towards Bill, 'he managed to tell us a good bit over the radio last night, and we put two and two together, and reckoned we'd better get going. So we got going and came over to this island as fast as we could. We found Joe's boat here, and signs of an early departure – stacks of dud notes in crates on the beach – and all kinds of other interesting documents.'

'How did you get here so quickly? There are no boats near on this coast,' said Philip.

'We've got a few fast motor boats of our own,' said Sam. 'We took two of them and came along here top speed, down along the coast. There they are.'

The boys turned, and saw two big and smart motor boats bobbing on the water near the cove, each one in charge of a mechanic. Nearby was Joe's own boat.

'As soon as we spotted that the gang had wound

up their business and were going to go off with their dud money, we saw our chance,' grinned Sam. 'So we posted a man at each of the shaft-holes – we didn't know which one the gang used, you see – and then, up one of them came the whole of the gang, one by one. And we got them nicely.'

'Just like you got us,' said Jack. 'That was smart work. What are we going to do now?'

'Bill Cunningham is head of this show,' said Sam, and turned an enquiring face to Bill. Bill looked at the boys apologetically.

'Sorry I had to give you a wrong name,' he said. 'But my own name is a bit too well known in some quarters to give away when I'm on a job of this sort. So I was just Bill Smugs to you.'

'You always will be,' said Philip. 'I shall never think of you as anything else, Bill.'

'Right,' said Bill, grinning. 'Bill Smugs I am. Now – what about getting these pretty gentlemen safely into the motor boats?'

The gang of fierce-looking men were pushed into the two boats. Jake still wore his black patch, but he glared so fiercely at Kiki with his one free eye that Jack called the parrot to his shoulder. If looks could kill, Kiki would certainly have died under that glare of Jake's. The man was remembering how the bird had been locked up instead of the boy. That mistake had probably led to all this bad luck.

'I think *we'll* sail Joe's boat home,' said Bill to the boys. 'Come on. Let the motor boats go first and then we'll follow. Hi, Sam! Make for that house – you know – Craggy-Tops. There's a good mooring-place there.'

'Right,' said Sam, and off the motor boats went, making a terrific roaring noise over the sea. Then Bill and the boys set off in Joe's boat, and all three boats went safely out of the gap in the rocks and on to the open sea beyond.

'Well, all's well that ends well,' said Bill, as they put up the sail and set course for home. 'But there *were* a few moments when I didn't think we were going to end up as well as we *have* done.'

The boys thought so too. Philip wondered how the girls were getting on. They would be worried by now.

'I'm jolly hungry,' said Jack. 'It's ages since I had a good meal – really ages.'

'It must be,' said Bill. 'Never mind – soon be back now – then you can tuck in to your heart's content.'

The girls and Aunt Polly heard the sound of the motor boats long before they came to shore. They went out to see what was making the noise. They were filled with astonishment to see two big motor boats packed with men, and a sailing boat which looked like Joe's, all making for Craggy-Tops.

'Whatever does it all mean?' said Aunt Polly, who was still looking white and ill. 'Oh dear! – my heart will never stand all this excitement.'

The motor boats nosed to the mooring-posts in the little harbour. The girls ran down, and were amazed to see Joe among the men. They stared at them, trying to find the boys.

'Hallo, there!' called Sam. 'Are you looking for Bill What's-his-name and the boys? They're following after us in the other boat. Have you got a telephone here, by any chance?'

'Yes, we have,' said Dinah. 'What are all these

men? Why is Joe with them?'

'Tell you everything soon,' said Sam, getting out
of the boat. 'I must telephone before I do anything.
You show me the phone, there's a good girl.'

Sam put through a call, asking for four or five
motor-cars to be sent to Craggy-Tops at once,
to take away the prisoners. Aunt Polly, her heart
beating fast, listened in the greatest surprise. What
could all this mean?

She soon understood when the sailing boat
arrived, and Bill and the boys came into the house.
They told her the whole story, and she sank back on
the couch in horror when she heard what a wicked
and dangerous fellow Joe was.

'As clever as a bagful of monkeys,' said Bill. 'But
he's not got away with it *this* time – thanks to these
four smart children.'

'It's funny,' said Jack. 'We went to the island to
find a Great Auk – and we found instead a whole
gang of men working at hidden printing-machines
down in the mines.'

'If I'd known you were doing things like that, I'd

have sent you all to bed,' said Aunt Polly severely. That made everyone laugh.

'Oh, naughty girl, naughty girl, Polly!' cried Kiki, flying to Aunt Polly's shoulder.

The cars arrived as the boys and Bill were in the middle of a most enormous meal. The men were packed into them and driven off swiftly. Sam said goodbye and departed with them.

'Good work, Bill!' he said as he went. 'And those kids want a pat on the back too.'

They got plenty of pats. The next day or two were so exciting that not one of the children slept properly at night.

For one thing they were taken to the nearest big town, and had to tell all they knew to two or three very solemn gentlemen.

'Big wigs,' said Bill mysteriously. 'Very big wigs. Jack, have you got the photograph of that pile of tins you saw on the island? Joe denies that he ever took supplies there, and we've found some empty tins in the cellar at Craggy-Tops which we may be able to identify by means of your snap.'

So even the little photograph of the tins came in useful, and was a bit of what Bill called the 'evidence against the prisoners'.

Another little bit of excitement was Jack's nugget. The boy was disappointed to hear that it was not valuable – but as a curiosity, a memory of a great adventure, it was thrilling.

'I shall take it back to school with me and present it to the museum we have there,' said Jack. 'All the boys will love to see it and handle it and hear how I got it. Won't they be envious! It isn't everybody who gets lost in old copper mines and finds a nugget hidden away. The only thing is – I'm awfully disappointed it's not valuable, because I did want to sell it and share the money between us.'

'Yes,' said Lucy-Ann, 'that would have been lovely. Tufty's share of it would have paid for his and Dinah's schooling, so that their mother and aunt could have had a rest, and not had to work so hard. It's a pity we couldn't have got a lot of money for it.'

But that didn't matter a bit, because, most unexpectedly, a very large sum came to the four children from another source. A reward had been offered to anyone giving information that would lead to the discovery of the counterfeiters – and it was naturally presented to the four children, though Bill had his share of it too.

Philip's mother came to Craggy-Tops when she heard all about the strange and thrilling adventure and its unexpectedly marvellous results. Jack and Lucy-Ann loved her. She was pretty and kind and merry, everything a mother should be.

'It's a shame your mother can't have a nice home of her own and you and Dinah with her,' said Jack to Philip.

'We're going to,' said Dinah, her eyes glowing. 'At last we're going to. There's enough money now for Mother to make a home for us herself, and stop working so hard. We've reckoned it all out. And what about you and Lucy-Ann coming to live with us, Freckles? You don't want to go back to your crusty old uncle and horrid old housekeeper, do you?'

'*Oh!*' said Lucy-Ann, her green eyes shining like stars. She fell on Philip and hugged him tightly.

Dinah never did that, but Philip found that he liked it. '*Oh!* Nothing could be nicer! We'd share your mother, and we'd have *such* fun together. But do you think your mother will have us?'

'Of course,' said Dinah. 'We particularly asked her that. She says if she's got to put up with two children, she might as well put up with four.'

'And Kiki too?' asked Jack, a sudden doubt creeping into his mind.

'Well, of course!' said Dinah and Philip together. It was unthinkable that Kiki should not live with them all.

'What's going to happen to your Aunt Polly and Uncle Jocelyn?' asked Jack. 'I'm sorry for your aunt – she oughtn't to live in this ruined old house, slaving away, looking after your uncle, being lonely and miserable and ill. But I suppose your uncle will never leave Craggy-Tops?'

'Well, he's got to now – and do you know why?' said Dinah. 'It's because the well water is salt. The sea did go into it, entering it from the old passage down there – so it's undrinkable. It would cost too much to put the well right, so poor old Uncle had to choose between staying at Craggy-Tops and dying of thirst, or leaving it and going somewhere else.'

Everyone laughed. 'Well, Joe did some good after all when he flooded the mines,' said Philip. 'It has forced Uncle Jocelyn to make up his mind to move – and Aunt Polly will be able to get the little cottage she has always wanted, and live there in peace, instead of in this great ruin – with no Joe to do the rough jobs.'

'Oh – that horrid Joe!' said Lucy-Ann, with one of her shivers. 'How I did hate him! I'm glad he's locked away for years and years. I shall be grown up when he comes out of prison, and I shan't be afraid of him any more.'

Bill arrived in his car, bringing with him a crate of ginger beer, for now no one could drink the well water. The children cheered. It was nice to have ginger beer for breakfast, dinner and tea. Bill presented Aunt Polly and Philip's mother with a most enormous thermos flask full of hot tea.

'Oh, *Bill*!' said Philip's mother, with a little squeal

that Kiki promptly imitated. 'What an enormous flask! I've never seen such a giant. Thank you so much.'

Bill stayed to supper. It was hilarious especially when Philip's mouse ran out of his sleeve on to the table to Dinah's plate. That made everyone laugh. Lucy-Ann looked round at the laughing company and felt glad. She was going to live with a grown-up she would love, and children she was fond of. Everything was fun. Everything had turned out right. What a good thing she and Jack had escaped from Mr Roy all those weeks ago, and run away with Philip to Craggy-Tops!

'It's been a grand adventure,' said Lucy-Ann out loud. 'But I'm glad it's over. Adventures are too exciting when they're happening.'

'Oh *no*,' said Philip at once. 'That's the best part of an adventure – when it's happening. I think it's a great pity it's all over.'

'What a pity, what a pity!' said Kiki, having the last word as usual. 'Wipe your feet and shut the door. Put the kettle on. God save the Queen!'

About the Author

Enid Blyton, who died in 1968, is one of the most successful children's authors of all time. She wrote over 700 books, which have been translated into more than forty languages and have

sold more than 500 million copies around the world. Her stories of magic, adventure and friendship continue to enchant children the world over. Enid Blyton's beloved works include The Famous Five, The Secret Seven, Malory Towers, The Magic Faraway Tree and the Adventure series.

The extraordinary number of books that Enid Blyton had published during her lifetime meant that she worked with several different publishers. However, Macmillan was undoubtedly one of her favourites. Enid Blyton published thirty-eight original titles with Macmillan, including the brilliant Adventure series – with *The Island of Adventure* in 1944 being the first book in this series about the exciting adventures of Philip, Jack, Lucy-Ann, Dinah and Kiki the parrot. Blyton is even quoted as saying '. . . *why do I have so many publishers? Why do I not have one only, and that Macmillan's.*'

Enid Blyton was a prolific letter-writer, and in 1990 a collection of some 400 autographed and typed letters was deposited at the British Library as part of the Archive of Macmillan Publishers Limited. A further deposit to the British Library in 2004 included a call-book showing Enid Blyton's visits to the Macmillan offices.

The letters of Enid Blyton provide us with a valuable insight into her writing career, particularly while writing the Adventure series, and her relationship with Macmillan Publishers. During this period it was reported that a Children's Editor was first appointed by Macmillan to manage the growing number of children's books, although it was not until 1979 that Macmillan Children's Books became a separate division under the directorship of Michael Wace. The following quotations come directly from letters that Enid Blyton wrote to G. J. Heath, Director of Macmillan:

'*I am quite prepared to do any children's books you like for Macmillan's, and you know that I would be proud to do them for you. You haven't many children's titles, and it would be lovely if I could give you some best-sellers.*'

The original books and jackets of the Adventure series were illustrated by (Cecil) Stuart Tresilian, who during this period was contracted to work exclusively for Macmillan, illustrating books. Evidence from Enid Blyton's letters shows her involvement in the artistic process and her enthusiasm for Tresilian's illustrations:

'*Let's get a tip-top artist, one who can really make the characters live.*'

'*Mr Tresilian has made the book twice as good with his interpretation of the characters, especially the parrot.*'

It seems that Tresilian was also passionate about the Adventure series, despite trying to fit illustrating them around his war efforts and his house being bombed. '*I am doing my best to get on with the plates but have been held up by the appalling condition of this house since the bomb*' – a great piece of social history! In a letter to Mr Heath regarding the last book in the series Stuart remarked about the stories, '*They are always good fun to do and very illustratable. I shall enjoy doing the drawings and will get them done for you as expeditiously as possible.*'

Enid Blyton – with the help of Tresilian's glorious illustrations – produced a brilliant and exciting series of mystery and adventure books, full of all the trademarks of her inimitable storytelling. She herself was clearly proud of what she had achieved.

'*I feel a bit excited about it as I have one of my "hunches" and feel we are at the beginning of a Big Thing!*'

'*It is a real thriller.*'

Enid Blyton's hunch was indeed correct as in 2014 *The Island of Adventure* celebrated its seventieth anniversary. The series went on to span eight titles, all of which continue to capture the imaginations of children to this day.